THE END OF LOVE

Translated from the Spanish by Katherine Silver

McSWEENEY'S

McSWEENEY'S
SAN FRANCISCO

WWW.MCSWEENEYS.NET

Cover art by Jon Contino

This Work has been awarded the International Short Story Award Ribera del Duero 2011, endowed by the Consejo Regulador de la Denominación de Origen Ribera del Duero.

ISBN: 978-1-938073-56-4

FIRST PRINTING

To my son, Juan, with all my love

CONTENTS

WE WERE SURROUNDED BY PALM TREES

. . . I REMEMBER WHEN IT STARTED. THERE IS ONE SCENE THAT comes back to me, frequently, though it seems arbitrary to focus on it.

Less than an hour of daylight remained. We put our suitcases down in a corner and looked around. The exotic poverty of our accommodations (less than one hundred square feet, a window covered with a burlap bag, and two old foam-rubber mattresses, each on a rickety wood-and-braided-rope bed) merited mention, but instead I spoke excitedly about the novelty of being alone:

"Too bad we have company."

"Keep your voice down. They can hear."

Marta was leaning over, looking for something in her suitcase, and I didn't reply until she had stood up.

"You forget they don't speak Spanish."

In one hand she was holding a colorful piece of fabric we had bought the day before, and in the other the mosquito net we had been using constantly since the beginning of the trip. She held it out to me.

"We don't know that for sure . . . Look at the bright side: if we hadn't joined them we might not have found a boat willing to take us."

"I don't like them."

"Admit it, you wouldn't have liked anybody."

Marta was standing next to one of the beds, scrutinizing me, the cloth unfolded but not yet spread out. I looked up at the ceiling, on her indication, where I saw a ring and understood what she wanted me to do.

"It's not that . . . " I climbed onto the bed and attached the mosquito net. "But it doesn't matter. We're lucky. This place is much more remote than I had imagined. Anything might happen."

"You've really changed . . . "

Marta had spread the cloth over the mattress, tucked in the corners, and, without checking on the result, had knelt down again to rummage around in her suitcase.

"What do you mean?" I asked, watching her stand up holding her toiletries.

"Nothing," she answered. "Just that you used to be a little more intrepid."

"Hey, first you criticize me for complaining that we're not alone, and now, when I accept that, it turns out I'm a chicken."

Marta smiled when she heard the word *chicken*, and I was happy to have chosen it. She had dumped her toiletries onto the bed where we would sleep and was separating out the bottles of insect repellent.

"I didn't like her attitude," I added. "It's not a good idea to get too friendly with the crew. Did you notice how the skipper was looking at her?"

It must have been there, in the ensuing silence, that I felt the first hint of what was to come. Marta didn't think it necessary to respond, and I didn't speak. There had been nothing, until that moment, particularly jarring—if anything, it was all fastidiously normal. Everything turned out so differently than we expected . . . The heat, the rain . . .

I think I should make some things clear. I have not even mentioned where we were. We were surrounded by palm trees. Night was falling. The landscape was covered with a thin milk-white film, but through it everything glowed in reddish tones: the earth, the monkeys who had followed us from the beach, people's faces, the rocks. There was no particular reason for us to be there. Every reason; none. What I mean is that we could have been anywhere. On a different continent, in a different sea. But we weren't. We were on an island in the Indian Ocean off the coast of Africa where we had just arrived from a neighboring island. The one we had left was outfitted with a small aerodrome, had tourists and bustling trade, whereas this one had almost nothing. To get to it, we had chartered one of the sailboats the local fishermen made available to tourists, usually for trips of no more than a few hours. It was less usual to hire one, as we had done, for more than a day. Hence we were obliged to join a previously arranged excursion. Disgruntled, I had not even bothered to find out how many people would be in our party. I tried to consider them as mere imponderables whom I intended to ignore—to render them, if possible, invisible. That morning on the quay, however, when I first saw our traveling companions, I felt somewhat unsettled. Disagreements, differences in judgment, could arise. Two days and two nights in unfamiliar circumstances is a long time, and in the end we would have to share something more than the solicitude of the sailors who were taking us and looking after us. Our plan was to visit the island's principal settlement, where—someone had told us—it was still possible to find antique furniture and other objects at bargain prices; we did not know what theirs was. It was early, the day had not yet dawned, and before they came into full view and I could discover for myself how many they were, Marta enlightened me:

"Good news, there're only two."

"Don't be so sure," I answered. "Two couples would have been better; they would have entertained each other."

My first impression was somewhat mistaken, stereotypical. He was German, originally Austrian, and probably around sixty-five years old. Neither the stiffness of his spine struggling to maintain good posture, nor the incipient defeat with which his neck, sinking between his shoulders, was beginning to surrender to the weight of his head, could go unnoticed. His body, on the other hand, was thin and wiry; his hair was gray and cut short, and his blue eyes were so lively and inquisitive that a less than astute observer might easily have guessed he was ten or fifteen years younger. Adding to this impression would be his manner and the way he dressed—not because this was informal or juvenile, which it was, but because it managed not to give the overwrought effect typical of people who dress young without being young. His clothes, the bag where he carried his passport, his sunglasses, and even the watch he wore on his wrist did not seem recently plucked from a shop window but rather really, truly, his. I did not ask his profession; it's possible he did not have one, that he plied various trades or enjoyed an alternative lifestyle as the founder or leader of some commune. The year 1968 was plastered across his forehead in California sun and iodine, as well as all the rust of who knows how many tons of Buddhist doctrine and "New Age" thinking, but at first I didn't notice that behind the traces of his generation's failure, the well-educated manners of a middle-aged lothario, his conciliatory and democratic spirit, there lay, in fact, a troubling anxiety, a reflection of the secret inhibition of the child he might have been, raised without a father amid the ruins of Dresden or Berlin. The woman with him, also German but of Indian origin, seemed for her part to be the stubborn product of her times, a woman who was heir to a variety of childhood traumas—moves, parents' divorce, her own beauty—that had turned her into a grown-up while she was still playing at being a bride and a heroine of a novel, and who, aware of her misfortune, had become wizened by her ill-conceived attempt to hold on to what she knew she had already lost. She was just over forty and could easily have been his daughter; in fact, through her demeanor of lover-nurse, lover-geisha, lover-confessor shone the devotion of a disciple. What was not immediately apparent was that behind her beauty, largely intact despite her cloying sweetness, the havoc wrought by an expansive though not necessarily voracious sexuality throbbed recognizably.

I did not have all these thoughts when I first saw the couple on the quay; they are the product of the chaotic impressions I collected during the trip. On the quay I was more puerile and prosaic; I noticed only the difference in their ages. And one other thing: both he and she ignored me and focused on Marta, as if they wanted to get at me through her or as if I held no interest for them at all.

The crossing took a long time because of the wind. We sailed in a zigzag down the tongue of the sea that separated the island we were leaving from the mainland; later, with the sail down and the help of poles, we navigated through the mangroves; and finally, when the wind turned in our favor, we reached the open sea—a total of eight hours, three more than planned. And this was thanks only to good luck, for the journey would have become even more difficult had we been taken unawares by a storm and forced to seek refuge on land. Luck and the crew—four sailors, their skin tinged with all the bloodlines of the Indian Ocean—who diligently carried out their duties. Among them only the skipper, slight and with long dreadlocks, spoke to us in a combination of English and Italian. His job, in addition to manning the till and managing his mates, consisted of helping them, each time he changed course, to move the boat's ballast from one side to the other. From the start, he had slipped into the conversation—along with the obligatory subjects meant to awaken our interest—subtle hooks with which to lull us into a false sense of camaraderie that, when employed in the service of a commercial transaction, especially in such a remote place, often has the sole purpose of multiplying the situations from which to extract profit. Be that as it may, he seemed neither violent nor conspiratorial, and when I realized that his questions were meant to gauge our tolerance for what he called "soft drugs," I was reassured that he simply wanted to roll a joint. What I didn't like was that our female traveling companion smoked with him. At first she had hesitated, turning to her partner as if to request permission, and he, who had declined to smoke a moment earlier, gave it to her with a wink.

In fact, this is what I was talking about hours later in the room where we would sleep when Marta felt obliged to defend them. After organizing the various medications, she had taken off her sandals and was putting on shoes that would better protect her ankles from the evening mosquitoes.

"Don't keep on about it . . . " she said cheerfully, though also sharply. "We've been lucky. They're normal. They haven't wanted to go anywhere else or proposed we do anything extravagant."

"I should hope not. We split the cost of the boat rental, and we agreed to return the day after tomorrow."

"We won't have any problems. You'll see."

Marta put an end to the conversation, but we had very nearly had our first conflict. That we had a place to stay at all was thanks to Marta, who, when we disembarked on the beach and saw the cabañas where the skipper intended for us to stay, had set out to look for a more comfortable alternative. The others hadn't refused outright, but they took their time deciding, and I know—because one intuits such things—that deep down they followed us reluctantly. I would even say that not only were they not averse to sharing quarters with the crew but they seemed quite pleased at the prospect. He, at least, was the one who seemed most eager to do so.

None of us now regretted it. And with good reason. Though precarious, the contiguous rooms we occupied were on the rooftop terrace of a house built around a courtyard with three palm trees, and from which we enjoyed an impressive view. The process of finding the place had, in itself, made the effort worthwhile. Dozens of children had come out to greet us as we approached the village, and they practically carried us there on their shoulders. The momentum of the crowd had swept us through the gate separately and, for a moment before the landlord saw me and the German, I had the chance to observe his expression of disbelief and fear when he saw the two women burst into his courtyard.

Marta clearly wanted to end the conversation, and I did not insist. She stood up from the bed where she had sat down to put on her shoes, smiled, and gave me a kiss. This was a more efficient means of changing the subject than pleading, than saying, *enough, let's focus on what matters*. And what mattered was for us to enjoy our much-needed African vacation. I don't remember if anything else was said; at that moment we heard a muezzin's call to prayer, then others joined in, and we stood there without moving. When they stopped, our traveling companion entered the room. She had put on perfume and substituted the dress she had been wearing on the boat for pants and a shirt. It was time to take her malaria pill, and she had run out of water.

"We'll have to buy more," Marta said, handing her our last bottle. "I guess we'll find some somewhere."

The German woman took the bottle, swallowed the pill, and stood there looking visibly ill at ease. I assumed she needed something she was ashamed to ask for in my presence, so I went out to wait on the terrace. Earlier, when we arrived at the house, we had agreed to split up the chores to best take advantage of whatever daylight remained: some would inform the village chief of our arrival, as we had been advised to do, and the others would return to the beach to tell the skipper that we had found another place to stay. When I proposed this division of labor, the German, wanting to provoke me or perhaps responding to a desire he did not know how to temper, quickly agreed, and suggested that the two of us pay the chief a visit, while Marta and his partner returned to the beach where we had left the sailors. Then he waited silently for my response, and although his rather grave expression did not even remotely suggest one, I chose to take it as a joke:

"Oh, yes, definitely, or we could just sell them straight away to the owner of the house for a couple of camels."

I had been absorbed for a while watching our host light a fire on the terrace when I heard a noise that made me look toward the highest part of the house—an open tower accessed through a stairway that began on the rooftop where I was standing. There he was again. His back was partially turned toward me, and he was looking over the handrail. I don't know how long he had been in that spot, but at least longer than I had been in mine. He was apparently unaware of my presence. He was engrossed, looking at something through binoculars. I went to stand next to him and looked in the same direction. A few seconds later, he pulled the glasses away from his face and placed them in front of mine. At first my eyes wandered aimlessly until, with his help, I discovered what he had been looking at. In one of the neighboring courtyards there was a water well, and next to the well, a very young girl—bare-chested—was washing her underarms. I immediately looked away, so perplexed I could not utter a word.

"It's too bad the women here are so inaccessible," he said as he took the binoculars from me and started looking through them again.

"What are you doing? Are you crazy?" I finally said. "Don't you realize that if somebody catches us, we could be in big trouble?"

"They wouldn't know what we were looking at. Anyway, the people here aren't that strict," he answered, casually lowering the binoculars. "It would be a problem in the city, but not in these small communities where almost everybody belongs to the same family. Haven't you noticed that the women don't cover their faces?"

I had noticed, yes. I had even seen more than one woman with her hair showing, and I had also noticed that the scarves of those who did cover their heads were brightly colored rather than black. But his explanation did not reassure me, nor could it have. I had also noticed that since our arrival, the women in the house had disappeared, and only the man was attending us. It frightened me to imagine what he would have been capable of doing had he found us spying on one of his own daughters rather than a neighbor's.

"It doesn't matter. Don't do it again," I charged him categorically.

Not wanting her to accuse me of always imagining the worst, I decided not to say anything to Marta when she and the German woman finally emerged from the bedroom.

I did ask her what had kept them so long. We had already separated from the Germans on the road to the beach and, following our host, were walking through the streets on the way to the home of the village chief. It was difficult to talk and avoid bumping into the many people around us, and Marta didn't answer. I was carrying the camera, but I did not take a single photo. I regret it. If I had, those photos would now be of what could have been. The house of the chief—a civil service position without any tribal significance—was outside the village, and we had to make quite a detour to get there. Along the way we passed places we would not visit again: a bend in the road where a solitary baobab grew; the ruins of an old mosque in front of which our host stopped, waiting for the photo we didn't take . . . I remember the throngs of children surrounding us, asking for money, and a column of young women, almost girls, carrying jugs of water on their heads, who stopped to look at us as we walked through a field.

The chief—a tall, ungainly, fifty-something man with a long face and yellowish, pockmarked skin—was eating in a shed attached to the main house with a friend who was every bit as tall. While recovering from his understandable surprise, he looked at Marta longer than was strictly necessary but promptly recovered his bureaucratic demeanor. We apprised him of the length of our stay on the island and declined his not very persuasive invitation to join them at the table; he promised to visit us that very night or the following day.

On the way back, soon after buying four bottles of water that our host refused to allow us to carry, Marta reminded me of the question she had left unanswered at the beginning of our walk. She did so unintentionally; neither her awareness of having postponed something nor, of course, any desire to encourage what she had for a while been calling my exasperating need for information had any part in it.

"It's odd. Don't you have the feeling you've met them before?"

"Who?"

"Christine and Paul."

This was the first time I'd heard the Germans' names since they had spoken them in the morning, when we'd met, and it took me a while to understand.

"No. Why?"

"I do. Especially her. I haven't been able to stop thinking about it since you left us in the room. She seems so fragile . . . "

I waited for her to continue and, when she didn't, I took the opportunity to ask if she had wanted anything in particular.

"No, nothing. We just talked. She told me about their trip and she asked about ours."

I was sorry Marta wasn't more explicit, but at that moment the crowd following us forced us to focus all our efforts on moving forward, and I missed the opportunity to inquire more deeply. Nor did I later, when we reached the house in the dark. We found our dinner spread out on a straw mat on the rooftop terrace. Our traveling companions were not there; they had not yet returned despite how close we were to the beach. We tried to wait for them, but it was impossible to make our host understand, and before we knew it, he had brought us a bowl of water to wash our hands and was serving us tea. Then he sat down with us and started uncovering the bowls of coconut rice, vegetables, and fish . . . The Germans' absence struck me as strange, and I actually started worrying that something untoward might have happened. In any case, reassured by Marta's apparent calm, I managed to forget them, focusing instead on our host, on his skill at picking out for himself the worst of each dish while making it clear, through the subtleties of his elaborate rituals of politeness, that he considered us his guests, above all. Twice he left to bring something from the kitchen.

"Did you notice the chief's friend?" Marta asked the first chance she had. "He was kind of scary."

I had just deduced, not without sadness, that in spite of how old he looked, our host must have been about my age, and I did not answer immediately. Moreover, something told me that Marta, as she did frequently, was merely trying to fill the silence.

"And him . . . " I answered. "I don't know if we did the right thing going to visit him. They looked like mafiosos."

It was not, however, until the next time we were left alone that Marta mentioned the Germans' lateness. She must have found it difficult, for it violated our perennial division of roles: my job was to worry, to ask questions, and hers to quell my doubts, destroy my sickly skepticism with her gushing vitality. I am the one who no longer hopes for anything and she the one who always hopes for more.

"Don't you think it odd that they haven't gotten back yet?"

She had just formulated the question when we heard two loud knocks. Moments later, the village chief appeared, preceded by our host. He had come, as promised, to return our visit, but as he was already informed that we were there with another couple, the first thing he did before sitting down was to ask us where they were. I sensed that he knew the answer better than we, and I told him what I knew.

"It is a little late to be at the beach," he answered. "This town is not as dangerous as others on the island, but it is not prudent."

He seemed to have carefully weighed his words beforehand: they deftly emphasized his authority and subtly exhibited his merits. After the less than gracious reception at his house, he had clearly been rehearsing his part on the way.

"Even so, they should have been back by now," Marta added. She was trying to show our friends in a good light, explain that nothing they were doing should take them much longer, but it sounded like an expression of concern.

Unexpectedly, our visitor ignored her words and focused on extracting information from us. He made use of our host, whom he was now translating, to disguise as casual what was nothing but a veiled interrogation. Once he had figured out who we were and what we were doing, he began to issue warnings. He began to draw, circuitously, a boundary between him and us, to put us in our place, to remind us of our condition as privileged tourists. It was not at all clear what he was looking to do: eventually receive a tip or sensitize us to the reality of the island. I did not, however, find any reason for alarm. He seemed to be one of those functionaries stranded in the provincial backwaters of almost nonexistent states whose loyalty is divided between his useless and youthful idealism and the necessary compromises forced on him by reality, but who, precisely for this reason, will never force reality, nor, by extension, would the corruption he facilitated ever go beyond a simple transaction (always hinted at, never demanded). The expression on his face when he took his leave made me wonder if that balance was beginning to falter.

"There are certain things people here don't understand. I see no problem with the two of you. But tell your friends. I wouldn't want anything to happen to the lady."

I didn't like the timing of his warning: too geometrical. But what I liked least of all, for it implied a certain suggestion of intimidation, was that he had no qualms about openly contradicting the relative indifference he had shown at the beginning of his visit when I had told him where our traveling companions were.

What things did the people there not understand? Returning home a mere hour late? Marta, who had not opened her mouth since her initial interjection, must have been asking herself the same question, for as soon as we were alone, she said we should go to the beach.

"Why?" I asked. "What will you tell them? I don't think we should get involved."

All told, we spent less than forty-eight hours on that island. Two days and two nights is a brief interval, but the best and the worst often happens in the shortest possible time. I cannot say exactly what, but something was going on between Marta and me, that much was clear. And whatever it was, it spoiled the time we thought would bring us closer. From that moment, as far as we were concerned, the die was cast: Marta was determined to follow her instincts without considering my reluctance, and I had a growing sensation that something (maybe only partially) unknown was threatening to swallow us up. I knew that Marta felt irresistibly interested in our traveling companions and, diffusely, as in a dream, *I* felt that her interest was piqued by how she thought they compared to us—an unusual feminine comprehension that, spurred on by what we euphemistically called our constant misunderstandings, defied all reason.

"You can wait for me here if you want," she said with determination. "We have to tell them, just so they know."

We started for the beach, led by our host, who lit our way with one of the oil lamps we had used while we were eating. Shortly after leaving town we caught sight of the glow of a bonfire, and soon we heard voices. We couldn't see them until we had climbed the dune at the edge of the beach. They had positioned the trunks of three palm trees around the fire and were accompanied by the skipper and one of the sailors.

"Look who's here!" the German exclaimed when he saw us appear out of the darkness. "You frightened us."

Whereas his girlfriend was smiling, apparently relieved by our appearance, the voice of our traveling companion sounded cloying and not very friendly. He seemed drunk. As it had been Marta's initiative to go there, I waited for her to respond, but she didn't. In the meantime, we had reached them and stopped in front of one of the angles of the imperfect triangle formed by the logs they were using as seats; the sailors, barely recognizable through the smoke and the darkness, sat on one, and the Germans each sat on one of the others.

"We were a little worried when you didn't show up to eat," I finally responded in Marta's silence.

I was about to explain that we had already eaten, but the German beat me to it by announcing that they had. He was sorry. The sailors had grilled some fish on the fire, and they simply couldn't resist. They thought we wouldn't wait for them. I said we hadn't, then he suddenly turned from me to our host.

"We don't need you, don't worry," he said. "Leave the lamp here and go home."

I remember what followed as a succession of still shots. I looked at him (a challenging glimmer in his eye), I looked at her (indecisive, ill at ease), I looked at the two members of the crew (the skipper: leaning over his knees, awaiting my reaction; the sailor: his head down as if he wanted to melt into the darkness), I looked at our host (indifferent to what was decided, the oil lamp crowned with a halo of mosquitoes), I looked at Marta (hesitant, intent), and at the very moment the German woman reached down to pick up a piece of fruit from the tray on the sand and, by doing so, immediately caught the attention of her partner as well as that of Marta and the skipper, I felt time expand and was certain I had missed something.

"The village chief paid us a visit," I said. "It seems he doesn't like you being here."

"He can join us, too, if he cares to," the German answered scornfully. "Have a seat. You probably haven't had dessert."

I attribute to Marta the decision to remain, a decision determined, I suppose, by something that I had managed to perceive in my vigilant state: while I was biting my tongue so as not to answer the German, the sailor left to go to the cabaña where his mates were sleeping, and the skipper fidgeted in his seat to make it seem like he was going to follow suit, though this initiative was immediately aborted by the German, who urged him to go sit next to his girlfriend. Marta circumvented this by rushing to sit next to her, and what happened next, before the chief appeared, belongs to the terrain of speculation, of the ineffable. Insinuations, words with double meanings, lewdness; the sensation that none of them felt comfortable with us being there, not even he who had insisted we stay; and, underneath, the scourge of a double tension: the first innate to any courtship, and more so if it be of such an anomalous nature as this seemed, and the second derived from our presence as witnesses. That Marta would risk taking part in this, moreover, continued to astonish me. In fact, it was the reason for my reluctance to accept what was happening, for my disbelief that, in spite of everything, she was staying. How could she be certain she wasn't intruding? I must admit that the German's role as instigator, though disconcerting, was more than clear. As was, likewise, the hedonistic opportunism of the boat's skipper. On the other hand, interpreting the German woman's manner did not turn out to be so easy. Her indecisiveness, her shyness, rather than a true reluctance to become involved in the game her partner was playing, could have been due to the intimidating effect of our presence. Obviously, if Marta's motivation was other than I imagined it to be . . . It did occur to me, yes. Why not? Kurtz's evil, the sound of the jungle. Isn't this what Conrad was referring to in *Heart of Darkness*? The invocation of the irrational as a useful solution. There are no guilty parties, only occult forces. But it so happens that these forces arise only when something unleashes them, a dissatisfaction or a sorrow, and if I dismissed, let us say, civilized hypocrisy (compassion, for example, or the longing for justice) to explain Marta's sudden interest in our traveling companions, I was forced to consider something . . . How can I say it? Something that nobody easily admits. Perhaps I was the one responsible for our marriage having reached that plateau where everything is too familiar? Yes, I suppose this is what I meant when I indicated that Marta's interest in the Germans was perhaps influenced by a comparison with us . . .

Nothing had been decided, no lines had been crossed, by the time the chief appeared.

"I hope I am not interrupting anything."

He had come to ask us to break up the gathering and, though his words were cautious, his rhetoric was less restrained than it had been a short while earlier at the house. I suppose he needed only a moment to become fully apprised of the situation, or he had intuited it beforehand.

Intimidated, the skipper decided to slip away, and now, suddenly devoid of plans, our traveling companion did not protest but rather limited himself to observing with resentful arrogance the man who was guilty of breaking things up and who was standing his ground. How can I describe it? It was a reciprocal challenge, a mutual X-ray that took in everything. It was a duel and a temporary armistice in which neither surrendered; what did take place, in any case, was a haggling over the terms of the dispute.

We returned to the house in single file: the German led the procession, then came his girlfriend, then Marta, and I brought up the rear. Nobody spoke. The loquacity, the euphoria, had vanished. It was a procession of penitents, and I the most contrite.

I remember it precisely as I have just described, but I imagine that nothing was so simple. What's simple is what can be explained in simple terms. Hunches cannot be explained; they are anticipatory sensations, and even when normal, they cannot be explained.

As soon as we reached our room, I asked Marta what by then seemed quite evident to me:

"Don't you think Christine was on the verge on going off with the skipper?"

Marta did not immediately deny it, though she took her time to answer and, when she did, she made clear that the idea had never crossed her mind.

"What nonsense."

"Come on, it was obvious."

"All I saw was that Paul and the skipper wouldn't have minded."

"She wouldn't have, either."

We were already in bed, and she did not respond. She merely turned her back to me. Then she tucked in her knees, curled up, sighed, and fell asleep. She did not hear the commotion that broke out in the next room. Perhaps she incorporated it into her dream. My own was agitated: we were on an island that was much smaller than the real one, but our backs were stuck together, and no matter how hard we tried, we could not see each other.

I awoke to the muezzin's first call to prayer, and, as Marta was still sleeping, I went out to the terrace, resigned to share a long wait with the German, who I assumed to be as early a riser as I. To my surprise, it was his girlfriend who had woken first. She probably didn't expect to find anybody up so early, and for a few seconds, she didn't notice me. She was on her way to the bathroom and when she saw me sitting on the mat where they had served us breakfast, she instinctively covered her face with one hand while with the other she held closed the long shirt she had been wearing the night before, which was now her only garment. When she returned (her face washed, her shirt buttoned), she sat down with me the way Arabs do, cross-legged, her knees pointing in opposite directions. For a moment the bottom of her shirt was pulled taut, exposing the darkness of her sex sheltered between her thighs like a sea urchin among rocks. The way she paused before starting to talk testified to her shyness, though otherwise she behaved like someone who had embraced a purpose and was determined to achieve it. For a while we talked about the weather, the mosquitoes, other trips, then she brought up the subject of the night before.

"Last night we were all a little drunk. Especially Paul. I guess the chief's appearance made you uncomfortable."

"To tell the truth, I wish he wouldn't watch us so closely."

I had assumed she would talk about the nighttime dispute, not what had happened at the beach, but I was not sorry, for my response seemed to encourage her.

"Yes, it's true. It's a drag to feel him breathing down our necks. I'm not worried for myself. I'm worried for Paul."

"Anyway, I would be worried for the skipper. The chief would never dare do anything to us, but he could get himself into quite a mess."

Immediately I regretted having spoken. I had been too direct, and Christine imputed as much by lowering her eyes.

"Why do you say that about Paul?" I said, backtracking.

She did not answer right away.

"He's not used to this kind of pressure. He is too free."

She was sounding me out. She looked up again, but now there was a suspicious gleam in her black eyes that made them look even more evasive. I thought it better to remain quiet. If she was about to absolve Paul of all guilt, I was not going to be the one to point out that her attempt at absolution already constituted an accusation. I was unsettled by the disparate mixture of elements she embodied: stereotypical Oriental candor alongside the most irritating Western foolishness, the lack of physical inhibition of a secretary from Hamburg who goes to nudist racing events in a body that seemed made for concealment and eroticism. My silence was effective: she brought one of the breakfast pastries to her mouth and, after chewing it slowly, continued to speak.

"He disconcerted me, as well, when we first met. He scared me." She paused and looked at me as if to gauge how closely I was paying attention. "I'm adopted. My family is wonderful but very conservative: four generations of Lutheran missionaries. It was difficult to reject the prejudices they had instilled in me, and I almost got lost along the way. I was a total mess when I met Paul. I was nothing, a wreck being passed around from hand to hand. He rescued me, helped me get centered."

"But you say he scared you," I replied.

"Yes, I didn't believe him. So many times I'd come across people who pretended to be something they weren't . . . Until he showed me that he asks for nothing that he himself doesn't give . . . The only problem is when he gets drunk. He loses his head and he doesn't realize that other people don't share his free spirit. That's why I'm worried about the chief. And I was worried about you two, until yesterday when I spoke with Marta."

Christine paused, but now she was smiling confidently rather than scrutinizing me. I wanted to ask her how Marta had reassured her, but I remained cautious. Moreover, I did not completely trust her. She had seemed intimidated at the beach. I simply nodded as she took another pastry and picked up where she'd left off.

"He's so generous and free that he wants us to have a child. He can't, but I'll have it and it will be as if it were his."

I had not recovered from this confession when I heard some movement in the courtyard. Christine also heard it and disappeared just moments before the clay-colored head of the chief appeared at the top of the stairs. I don't know if he saw her. He didn't mention her, and I don't think he would have failed to take advantage of the opportunity. In fact, he seemed somewhat disappointed at finding me alone. He pretended this was just a casual visit, but it wasn't long before he revealed his purpose. Perhaps not his real one, but at least the only one he could put forward. He dispensed with insinuations and addressed it head on: he would not allow the events of last night to be repeated, he told me. If it were just Marta and me, there would be no problem, but the behavior of our traveling companions . . . Though I had nothing to do with it, I felt obliged to tell him that they had done nothing inappropriate. He did not contradict me; he didn't need to: he had delivered his message and I had received it. Shortly after the chief left, the German emerged from his room, without any traces of the previous night on his face; as if they had timed it, Marta appeared at the same moment, though she was blinking, stunned by the light, and, like Christine, dressed in the same clothes she had slept in. She seemed to be in a good mood, the memory of our misunderstanding buried, but, just in case, I let her eat breakfast and turned my attention to our traveling companion. He was elated, exclaiming his joy at the clear skies with an emphasis that disturbed me and that I associated with our forced nocturnal march from the beach and the shouting I had heard from his room after Marta had fallen asleep.

"Oh, I'm sorry I missed him," he said when I told him of the chief's visit. "Maybe I'll go see him. It's never a good idea to be on bad terms with authority."

We had agreed that they would take the boat and go for an excursion to another part of the island and that we would remain in town to find out if it was still possible, as we had been told, to buy antiques at bargain prices; pleased that we were going to spend some time without him, I did not respond.

When Marta was ready and we finally left, we crossed paths with the skipper on the stairs. He had come to find out our plans for the day. He was glowing, his hair greased back, but his gait was wary, fearful. After saying good-bye, we wandered through the streets of the medina for four or five hours without our host and followed by a crowd of children even larger than the one the previous day. As Christine had not showed her face again and Marta had not asked me about her, I preferred not to recount the conversation we had had. I did tell her about the chief's visit, but I did not give her many details nor did I mention the rivalry I was beginning to intuit between him and the German. I was afraid that she, prey to renewed suspicions, would choose to return sooner than planned. I think that was all there was to it. We accepted invitations from men and women who performed elaborate ceremonies to try to sell us junk—nothing worth buying except a copper teapot from an old woman at the door to her house—and we ended our excursion with a visit to an abandoned madrasa and two palatial mansions that retained from the splendor of their past only their sun-filled courtyards and the plumb lines of their walls. When we started back, the sky was totally overcast and there were flashes of lightning. We didn't speak, I suppose because it was exhausting to try to make our dejection at again suffering from the lethargy of waiting look like disappointment at the scantiness of our spoils. Instead of reconnecting spontaneously and lightheartedly as had been our goal for this trip, of suspending time, we were once again waiting. We were sharing the wait, but not for this was there less of a disconnect, for we were each, apparently, waiting for different results. Among other things, I can't explain why Marta agreed to accompany me that morning. A palliative for the way she had ended our nocturnal dialogue? An attempt to exorcise, by belittling it, the threat she sensed was hovering? A misstep? A mistaken assumption that she would find the confirmation of her fears sheltered in the night?

By the time we reached the house, the first drops of rain were already falling. We found our host on the terrace, moving the food to a dry spot. He welcomed us somewhat coldly and continued his task in silence until Marta entered the bathroom. Then he stopped and walked over to me.

"The other man said not wait them."

It seemed like he was trying to insinuate something, but this might have been a mistaken impression resulting from his hopeless English.

"What do you mean?" I asked.

"He no eat here."

"And she?"

"I no know."

"Are they still out on the boat?"

"No, boat on beach."

Marta came out of the bathroom before I had fully absorbed the strange information the host had given me. If they weren't on the boat, where were they? Not in town, for we had just come from there.

"What did he tell you, what's wrong?"

Marta stood at the door of the bathroom and looked at me. Though I was still not sure of the implications, I would have liked to hide from her what I had just learned.

"Nothing, it just seems like our friends have already returned from their excursion and don't want to join us for dinner."

"Where are they?"

"No idea . . . Maybe they got caught in the rain and took refuge in one of the cabañas on the beach," I ventured.

"Let's go."

"Don't be ridiculous. It's raining."

"I'm not ridiculous."

"It's absurd," I answered. "Think about it. They are adults."

This time it was Marta, still standing at the bathroom door, who paused, as if she were pondering something; then, bent forward to protect herself from the rain, she walked over to the low roof where our host had just laid out our lunch. She asked him to repeat what he had told me, which he did as awkwardly as before. Oddly enough, Marta sat down on the mat, apparently satisfied with the explanation. Obviously, I didn't point out to her that our host had given an excuse only for the German man's absence. The mere possibility that this had been deliberate increased my unease. I thought of the German's disconcerting courtship of the skipper; I thought of his defiant attitude toward the chief; I thought of his odd fixation, of Christine and our morning chat; of Marta and me, of the shipwreck of our longed-for vacation; of the rain.

We ate the same food we had eaten the night before, and our host repeated his hypertrophic rituals of hospitality. He no longer felt the need, however, to engage us in conversation, and ate in silence, nodding to encourage us to help ourselves when he offered us a dish.

Uncomfortable, Marta and I also didn't speak. I think we were both grateful for the presence of a stranger precisely because it exempted us from conversation, conscious of the qualms that kept coming between us, like invisible barriers, to the rhythm of the beating rain. It was not until we were finally alone after we finished eating that I attempted to break through, making a joke about the old woman from whom we had bought the teapot in the morning. She let a few seconds pass, then used the opportunity to confront what neither of us had been able to get out of our heads.

"We have to go look for them."

"Marta, it really doesn't make any sense."

"How can you be so sure? Something's wrong. It's not normal . . . "

She had blurted it out, as if by speaking quickly her concerns would carry more weight, and I forced myself to answer her slowly, perhaps excessively so:

"They told us the boat is at the beach. Nothing has happened to them. They must have stayed to eat with the crew."

We were facing each other, the mat between us, but our eyes did not meet. Marta looked up only when she was speaking, and every time she did so, I deliberately looked away. We behaved like two castaways who avoid looking at each other so as not to recognize their own situation in the other's eyes.

"I don't trust him. I'm afraid he'll do something."

"To whom? Christine?"

Marta nodded, almost ashamed, and I was unable to see how much surrender that gesture contained, how pleading it was.

"Oh, come on!" I exclaimed. I wanted her only to think things over; and I wanted to protect her from herself and me, to dispel once and for all the fog that was enveloping us, for her to focus on us.

Marta looked back at the mat, and, knowing I was starting down a path from which I could not turn back, yet unable to stop myself, I added:

"She's no saint, either. Whatever he does to her, she deserves it."

Marta did not react immediately. For a few seconds she kept her head down, engrossed in the rain pounding on the terrace full of puddles, then she raised it and said sharply:

"Don't say that again. You don't know her, and you have no right to judge her."

"And you know him?" I asked her.

"It's not the same," she answered. "He's different, don't you realize? He's a manipulator, a provocateur . . ."

"A moron, yes," I interrupted. "But so is she. We can't excuse her just because she's younger."

"Don't say that. It's not the same. He has no scruples, and she is at his mercy, just look at her."

"Yeah, right, the same old story of feminine weakness."

I said it without thinking, but the moment I did so I realized that I had transgressed an unwritten law when speaking about others—not to generalize. Marta's accusation was contained in the silence she kept while she considered the implications of my comment, and I took a daring step forward in an attempt to dilute it.

"I don't think we're so liberal after all. All that feminist nonsense and look where we end up."

"Don't make fun of me," Marta responded. "That has nothing to do with it. We are talking about one specific case."

"Of course we are talking about one specific case. That's precisely the point. We don't know anything about them."

"Look, I don't know why I'm scared, but I am. I can't help it. What do you want me to do?"

"She's an imbecile."

"Don't talk like that."

"But she is."

Marta looked at me, her eyes filled with anger.

"Maybe she is, but she needs help."

"Then what? What will happen when we are no longer there to protect her? Really, Marta, it doesn't make any sense. Think about it."

"For you, nothing ever makes any sense. Except your orderly life, your habits, your apathy. I can't stand it anymore. I feel like I'm suffocating."

This time, Marta didn't look down; she didn't need to. She cracked a bitter, scornful smile and stood up. As she crossed the flooded terrace and disappeared into our room, I became fully aware of the gulf that had opened up between us. I went after her, imagining that she would be getting ready to go out and look for the Germans, and I was prepared to not stop her, to even encourage her, but I found her on the bed, wet as she was, barricaded under the thick mosquito net.

"How awful, what a way to rain."

My intention had been to reconstruct a bridge between us, but Marta didn't answer. She didn't even look at me. What for? she must have been thinking. I tried again with another remark, and she still didn't respond. I tried once more, and the result was identical. Marta was mute. Marta wasn't speaking. Marta's entire demeanor had been transformed.

It is well-known that one of memory's most powerful tendencies is to identify those moments when it would still have been possible to change the course of events. Perhaps this explains why this scene in the bedroom with Marta is, along with our arrival on the island, the one from our trip that most frequently comes back to me. Almost twenty-four hours had passed since Marta had spread a piece of cloth over the bed where she was now lying. What would have happened if I had known how to say the right words rather than the unfortunate ones I had said? What would have happened if I had taken the initiative in time instead of pursuing a reconciliation devoid of substance? I can't help thinking that at that point, everything had already been decided.

An hour later we still knew nothing about our traveling companions. The rain—dense, warm, torrential—had not stopped. We continued drifting on our life raft. Our gestures were more sullen, more anguished; both of us were more reluctant to recognize ourselves in the other, despairing at ever being able to shout *Land*! When the words returned, weak and halting, when their volume, though slight, allowed us to improvise a sail, Marta emerged from under the mosquito net, took a jacket out of the suitcase, held it over her head with both hands as a precarious canopy, and with great determination went out into the rain. I did not try to stop her, nor would she have let me. Fortunately, our host had an umbrella, and thanks to my having taken the initiative to ask him for it, I could inflict my company upon her. We went through the gate, left behind us the labyrinthine streets of the village, climbed the dune, and when we looked down to the beach, I was relieved to see that the boat was, in fact, anchored there.

The reprieve didn't last long. We found the crew taking refuge from the rain in the first cabaña we came to, but, just as I had feared since I had conversed with our host, the Germans were not there. The skipper, who came out to greet us, told us that in the morning they had all gone out in the boat with the chief of the village and that when they felt the threat of the storm, they had returned, that the Germans had then gone off with him, he did not know where, though he had assumed it was to meet up with us.

"They aren't with us," Marta rushed to clarify.

"Did something happen?" I asked, surprised that the chief's hostility would have dissolved to the point of him having wanted to join the morning boat trip.

The skipper instantly caught on to the reason for my surprise and took the liberty of expressing some irony.

"No, they are now the best of friends."

I noticed how upsetting this was for Marta. Confused, she walked into the cabaña to confirm that what the skipper had said was true, and when she reappeared I suggested we go to the chief's house. How clueless I was, how arrogant. I felt so smug, believing victory to be within reach, and foolishly I offered her too late what a mere hour earlier would have been a salve. It was unnecessary, reckless. I don't think even Marta would have dared propose it. In spite of that, I did not have to insist.

We left the skipper and started off in the direction of the chief's house. It was not easy. We got lost several times, and several times I was on the verge of giving up. Several times I had the presentiment that the

German and Christine were not far away, but we did not cross paths with them or anybody else. We didn't speak, and we didn't exchange a single word more than was necessary at each fork in the road where we had to decide which direction to take. Finally, after an hour or more of wandering through the hamlet on the outskirts of the village, we happened upon the house. If I persevered, it was for my sake, not Marta's. I saw myself at the end of the road, offering her compassion and thereby guaranteeing peace and quiet in the coming days.

The shed where the chief and his dinner companion had greeted us the night before was locked. We called out, but nobody opened. We had better luck at the house, where a woman appeared shortly after we knocked on the door. She seemed frightened, did not speak English, and barely gave us the opportunity to explain who we were. For a while already we had been hearing the chorus of muezzins in the mosques of the village; it had stopped raining, the darkness of the night was edging out the last rays of the sun, we were soaking in spite of the umbrella, and the truth is we probably didn't inspire much confidence. She shut the door as soon as she could, and Marta and I stood there paralyzed. Before deciding if we should knock again or just give up, we heard a sound from the shed. Somebody had approached it from behind the house and was trying to open the door. We were startled. I think both of us would have run and hid, but each was waiting for the other and incapable of moving on our own. We were still in the same spot when, after entering the shed briefly and then leaving and closing the door, the chief of the village came around the corner of his house. He seemed agitated and it was obvious that he was not expecting to see us.

"Oh, it's you," he said, recovering from the surprise.

"And our friends?" Marta asked.

The chief didn't answer. He brought his right arm to his cheek, as if wanting to dry it with the cuff of his shirt, and climbed the stairs to the narrow front porch. When he reached us, Marta and I stepped down, leaving a space free in front of the door.

"You are wet," he said, then brought his sleeve back to his clay-colored cheek. "Wait while I bring you a towel."

Thanks to his last observation I realized that he wasn't wet, except for his brown city shoes, which he was wearing with bare feet. I think Marta also noticed this, and she repeated her question, now more nervous.

"Our friends? Did something happen to them?"

For the first time, he seemed impatient.

"No, nothing. Why?"

He had turned his back to us and was opening the door to his house with a key he had removed from a hiding place in the adobe wall.

"We went out sailing this morning, but we had to return because of the rain, and they ate here," he said, nodding in the direction of the shed. "They left a while ago, when it stopped raining. I accompanied them halfway."

He had managed to open the door, but rather than enter he turned and stared at us, standing up very tall, as if wanting to confront any possible suspicion surrounding his sudden friendship with our traveling companions. He looked like a giant. Behind him, in the shadow of the house, I saw the bright flickering of a fire, and a pair of eyes observing us through the darkness. I also thought I saw, though

I cannot be certain, a damp purplish gleam on his cheek that he rubbed twice with his shirt sleeve.

We didn't wait for him to give us a towel. Marta asked him to tell us the shortest way back to our lodging, he gave us the directions, and we left him just as he was inviting us to stay for dinner and offering to accompany us later, as he had with the Germans.

I don't remember anything about our return except that it was Marta who led for most of the way and that again we mostly kept silent. We walked quickly, almost ran. We got lost, but not as often as on the way there. I don't know what I was thinking about. I wasn't asking myself any questions. I wasn't thinking about either the Germans, Marta, or myself. I had the sensation that my triumph had been ephemeral, that it had never actually been mine, nor Marta's perhaps, and I simply followed her without thinking about anything or feeling worried about what she was thinking, if she was expecting anything from the future or if she believed we had one. Our fragile lifeboat had sunk, and we were again on our island, again with our backs to each other.

It was night when we reached the gate. Our host opened it for us.

"Your friends have just arrived," he announced, addressing me, as usual.

We climbed the stairs almost at a run, and when we reached the rooftop, there the two of them were, sitting on the mats where Marta and I had already become accustomed to keeping our differences at bay by waiting, impatiently, for them to arrive. He smiled smugly whereas she, her hair over her face, seemed to me to have one of her index fingers in her mouth, as if she were removing a hangnail or cleaning a wound with her spit.

"You see there was nothing to worry about?" I whispered to Marta.

Much later in bed, I wanted to hug her but she slipped away.

CAPTIVES

THE FIRST TIME I MET GUILLERMO CUNNINGHAM, INNOCUOUS in itself, was after a family Christmas Eve dinner; I was still sitting at the children's table and he showed up for dessert to pick up my cousin Alicia. Until twenty years ago, when the generational relay ushered in new traditions, three branches of my father's family—my family, with my grandfather at the head, and those of his two brothers with their respective offspring—would gather at the home of an aunt. A polyhedral army of legal and blood relations comprised each year of parents, grandparents, siblings, uncles, cousins, brothers-in-law, and parents-in-law . . . carrying out a sort of self-affirming ceremony with no purpose other than to establish continuity with times gone by when these multitudinous gatherings occurred with greater frequency, when the family had the resources to pay for them without incurring any hardship that would diminish the scant joy they provided. Not counting the very young and those like me who had recently emerged from adolescence, I think there were no fewer than forty pairs of eyes poor Guillermo Cunningham had to face during his official introduction, forty pairs of eyes and an equal number of ears listening attentively to his horrified stammers. They did not make things easy for him at all. My cousin Alicia, the only member of the family who did not attempt to mitigate the sharp awareness of the family's decadence with insufferable affectation, lacked the character to prevent her courtship from becoming the subject of discussion, this despite the fact that the person she had chosen surpassed with flying colors the expectations of those who claimed the right to judge him. Guillermo Cunningham had more money, more status, and was definitely more sophisticated than any member of our family, the only strike against him being a foreign surname that conjured vague social origins, as vague as the origins of his wealth—an indeterminate amount of income from nobody knew where and that would most likely not be increasing due to his lack of interest in business, which was an even more serious concern. I don't think, in any case, that it would have occurred to Alicia's parents, nor to any other adult relation, to in any way hinder their engagement. The possibility of bringing into the family someone who possesses wealth is much more tempting for those who have had it and no longer do than for those who never have. No, the battle they were waging was as paltry as it was simple: it was a question of raising their own value, vindicating themselves, selling their merchandise at a higher price. One had to make things difficult for the buyer, cannibalize him, force him to take on as his own the family's defects, embrace the family in its entirety and not even dream of creating a separate unit. And, of course, the less blood they shared with Alicia, the greater their objections, which spun into the realm of the ridiculous when it came to Alicia's uncles and grand-uncles, and diminished to mere symbolism when it came to her parents, the exception being our grandfather, the one most willing to remain entrenched in the rancid pride of the hereditary caste of traditionalists the men of his family had belonged to until the middle of the third decade of the twentieth century. Guillermo Cunningham not only did not have a profession but he had a Protestant surname that inevitably made him suspicious, this in spite of the firmness with which Alicia would hastily assert, whenever anybody brought the subject up, that his family had been Spanish and Catholic for three generations.

But the purpose of this story is not to relate the difficulties Guillermo Cunningham faced in achieving his goal of marrying Alicia, even if these would have discouraged a less persistent suitor. He had to employ infinite patience in order to untangle the many bonds that held Alicia captive. He had to smother his qualms, silence his own opinions about almost everything, and even nod in agreement with some he did not share; submit to others' customs and make his peace with social conventions that today would be laughable. He had to play the role of the fiancé at every family baptism and wedding, at every Christmas Eve dinner to which, as in the case of the occasion on which we met him, he invariably arrived for dessert and was allowed to take Alicia away for only a few hours. He had to hide who he was, pretend. He had to learn to watch her get dressed at dawn and go out into the cold night, make do with the promise of remote weekends when she would dare to invent a lie so she could stay with him, and improvise graceful exits from awkward situations. He had to leave floral tributes at the shrine in the town we came from, submit to an interrogation by the family's spiritual advisor, and, once he had finally complied with all the requisite rituals, he had to get married in a ceremony during which, in addition to sitting through the priest's contemptible political harangue, the four guests on his side found themselves buried under more than two hundred of us on Alicia's.

It is not surprising, given the circumstances, that when their lives were joined and nobody could prevent it any longer, Guillermo would take Alicia as far away as possible. At that time I was not kept informed of the affairs of the grown-ups, but echoes reached me of some attempts by the family to convince Alicia that, since Guillermo was not willing to put his fortune to any good use, she at least should use his money to start a business. This was not, obviously, a disinterested suggestion. It was informed as much by the ambivalent family pride, averse to Alicia becoming a kept woman, as by the possible advantages such an initiative would make available to other members of the clan. I don't know which of the many propositions ever passed beyond a speculative airing at gatherings where Alicia was not present, and which were proposed to her. It was suggested, I remember, that she start a plant nursery, a clothing shop, a furniture store, an antique shop, and even that she should resurrect the old family factory. As far as I understood it, Alicia did not seriously consider any of these suggestions, hence it is highly likely that they never even reached Guillermo Cunningham's ears; though I do know that someone considered approaching him directly, alarmed by the excuse Alicia put forth to reject them: her intention to study, as had always been her desire, so she could teach literature in high school. Alicia repeated this to whomever cared to listen, and nobody doubted that upon their return from their honeymoon, this is what she would do. Not even she could foresee how long the journey would last.

The day before she left, we all gathered for afternoon tea at her place, an apartment near the Royal Palace that Guillermo had bought a few months before the wedding. Claiming it was a wedding present for Alicia, he had declined to show it to anybody. In this way he had hoped to guard against unsolicited advice on the decor, and, judging from the results, he had been thorough enough to leave no room for any meddling. Not only did it contain all the necessities, but each element had been placed with a view to comfort that, because of its sobriety, was not susceptible to alterations without altering the explicit aesthetic out of which it arose. It is probable that if Guillermo had opted for a more variegated decor, such as the one he chose for what would be his last home, the final result would have been less resistant to interference. This was, on the contrary, a finished work, wholly self-contained, and precisely for this reason difficult to question even by those who did not share his refinement. I think that the silence it provoked in my family—a mixture of confusion and fear of not saying the right thing—was the only recognition Guillermo Cunningham ever received. In spite of her natural elegance, even Alicia seemed intimidated, lost in somebody else's strange interior. It was the first time she had played the role of hostess, and she had planned everything meticulously, torn as she was between two irreconcilable goals: showing off to her parents and pleasing Guillermo. This duality was reflected in the composition of the tea service itself: on the one hand, elements typical of a traditional Spanish tea service, such as chocolate, *torrijas*, *picatostes* . . . and on the other: biscuits, sandwiches, and tea. Besides an overabundance of food, the main consequence was that Alicia spent all her time shuttling back and forth between the kitchen and the living room. On one of those trips, she asked me to accompany her. Ever since she had discovered that I was the only one among her younger cousins who shared her love of reading, she would take me aside and interrogate me about the books I was reading and regale me with ethereal glimpses of a greater intimacy. Thanks to these moments, and in spite of the seven years that separated us, we had laid the foundation for one of those friendships—not devoid of a certain amount of innocent flirtation—through which an adult exerts her influence over someone younger by boosting his confidence and offering herself as a point of reference. It would not surprise me if Alicia, so deliciously conscientious, saw herself in this role as a sculptor who, wielding a chisel, is intent on removing from a stone slab everything that would have concealed its true morphology. What she surely never suspected was how often I longed to carry the myth of Pygmalion to its ultimate consequences and become her Galatea. That afternoon she lured me into the kitchen with the excuse of adding water to the kettle, but it was obvious that her goal was to show me that I could continue to count on her despite her new status as a married woman. After the customary questions about what I had been reading, she spoke of the journey she was about to embark upon. She had already done so in the living room before a larger audience, but whereas then, just moments before, she had been obliged to emphasize her final destination—New York—where she would stay for half of the four months they would remain abroad, she now gave me a detailed account of the long list of places she would visit on the way there. She promised to write and warned me that during that first stage she would not be able to receive my letters, but that once she was settled in New York, she expected me to write to her regularly. The way her eyes lingered warmly over me when she stopped talking and kept smiling, as if she hoped to retain my image in the retina of her green eyes, is the most vivid memory I have kept from that afternoon, the one that best summarizes the era it brought to an end. We hurried back to the living room, plagued by a sense of how inconsiderate we had been of Guillermo. Whereas I sat down, Alicia preferred to stand behind his armchair. She affectionately rested her hands on his shoulders, and he responded with a brief caress. He seemed calm, but the slight movement of his crossed leg indicated the opposite. The conversation turned to the house, which someone judged to be a bit small, and several voices, excited by having found something about which they could express their disapproval, concurred.

"Well, anyway," Guillermo defended himself, "it is just a pied-à-terre."

"What about when you have children?" somebody insisted.

"What do you mean, a pied-à-terre?" Alicia asked.

Alicia kept her promise, and I was soon receiving postcards from almost all the places they visited, as well as a few letters. The postcards all conformed to the same pattern. Although they were addressed to me using my family nickname and the closings were particularly affectionate, it was obvious that she wrote them along with many others, probably while sitting with Guillermo in a café. In them she told of her current whereabouts, mentioned some place she had visited or planned to visit, and closed with a quip about their next destination. Sometimes she substituted the quip for something unequivocally dedicated to me and on which she had clearly lavished more attention, as when she sent me from Yale a portrait of F. Scott Fitzgerald with Zelda and ended the text with: *From this side of paradise, Alicia,* or when from Pennsylvania she informed me that she planned to take the same night train that Holden, the young man in *The Catcher in the Rye*, had taken when he ran away from high school to New York City. Usually, however, she saved such details for her letters. These were short, written on sheets torn out of a spiral notebook, and before her trip was extended I did not receive many, perhaps only four or five. I remember one in which she complained about the humid heat of the South, and she added—invoking *Other Voices, Other Rooms* and *The Heart Is a Lonely Hunter*—that she now admired Capote and McCullers even more; but above all I remember another in which she drew parallels between her rambles along the highways of the United States and those of Lolita with Humbert Humbert. I remember this because I had just finished reading Nabokov's novel, and the whole time I was reading it I never stopped picturing Alicia as Lolita and Guillermo Cunningham as Humbert Humbert. Unfortunately, I no longer have any of those letters, which in any case did not otherwise nurture such fantasies. As far as I can remember, they were normal letters, rushed and happy like those of any newlywed taking the first long trip of her life and whose only defect is that she loves too many people so very much. If there was anything peculiar about them, it was the constant movement revealed by the postmarks. And, of course, the ones she began to send from New York, to my parents and to me when they finally arrived in that city, were no less predictable. For the first few days, they were ritually exclamatory; she dashed off details about her daily life, descriptions of the house where they were living, the routine they were starting to establish, the people they met; and they became more and more sluggish and laconic as her subject became less an account of the outside world, what she was seeing and discovering, and more what she was feeling and thinking. Given that they had not fixed an exact date for their return, Alicia did not feel compelled to give an explanation for the delay when the two months they had planned to be in New York had passed; instead she waited for echoes of the family's growing concern to reach her from Spain. Not even then was she able to offer a convincing reason, perhaps because the decision was not hers. Her mentions of Guillermo, which until then had been scant, began to abound (*Guillermo wants, Guillermo says, Guillermo needs*) at the same time as her excuses for further putting off her return proliferated, and suddenly, in a most natural way, she made it understood that she would not be returning for good, just for a visit, during the Christmas holidays or the following summer.

What did Guillermo want, what did he say, what did he need? Alicia never specified. Soon thereafter she brought up Columbia University and mentioned the possibility of both of them going to graduate school, then she made reference to Guillermo's fondness for film and the visual arts, or alluded to his intention—not for monetary gain, needless to say—to make use of his vast contacts to either work as a *scout,* as they call it in English, for Spanish galleries and publishing houses who need to know what is going on in New York, or as a consultant for Spanish organizations interested in holding events in the United States or establishing offices there. Something was shifting inside Guillermo, Alicia seemed to be telling us, though she never specified which of his different projects subsequently took on more significance, which he intended to tackle first. Nor was she explicit about herself. She said she still planned to become a teacher, and once she even announced that she had begun to study for her entrance exams, but, to tell the truth, this seemed unlikely.

In the meantime, our relationship languished. When it was settled that she would remain in the United States to live, the frequency of her letters diminished until they stopped altogether. If it is difficult to maintain an epistolary relationship over an extended period of time, it is that much more difficult to do so with someone who is no longer predictably as you remember them. I was no longer a child when Alicia had left, but the certainty that I would have undergone some kind of transformation since the day of the gathering at her house must have undermined her confidence in her ability to bridge, through letters, the generation gap between us. It is likely that I contributed to this by allowing a similar insecurity to contaminate my last letters. It is strange how quickly we both assumed that we would have to wait in order to reestablish our old complicity. Be that as it may, she stopped writing me, and instead I began to receive, through third parties, insistent invitations to come visit her in New York. I was not able to comply for some time, so I had to make do with conflicting reports I heard from her parents and siblings; the former were leery of her life with Guillermo, which they judged to be extravagant, and the latter were admiring and bewildered. Before I could judge for myself, I saw her twice at Christmas while she was visiting her family in Madrid; on both occasions it was too brief and there was too much going on for anything to take hold between us. The Alicia I glimpsed at these events had hardly changed at all in her compulsive desire to please and in her constant devotion to others, though an indefinable composure made her longing to remain invisible—go unnoticed, fade into the background—more difficult to achieve than in the past. In addition, however, to attributing this composure to her new worldly experiences, which had given her greater confidence and ease, I suspected—and for proof I would have to wait for my trip to New York—that this was not an expression of true serenity, the remnants of her old lack of guile having been polished and strengthened, and more a mask one dons when embarking on a process of self-renunciation and beginning to intuit its sinuous pathways. We knew nothing about Guillermo. Either he did not accompany her to Madrid or he excluded himself from her family obligations.

I arrived in New York one year younger than Alicia had been when she married Guillermo Cunningham, and I obviously did not make the trip for the sole purpose of visiting them. Alicia was providing me with a jumping-off point from which I could get to know the city, and my primordial urge was to take full advantage of it. I do not think she expected anything else.

I met her as I was exiting the customs area at JFK; she was holding a bouquet of flowers, which she gave me after hugging and kissing me effusively.

"Guillermo decided to stay home, but he is thrilled you're here."

She seemed happy to see me. It was Christmas Eve, and they had invited some friends over for dinner. Nervous, and without stopping to catch her breath, she continued talking and asking me questions as we walked to the parking lot, where she said a friend was waiting for us.

"We have a car," she explained, "but it is very old, a Bentley, almost a museum piece, and I don't dare drive it. Guillermo does."

It was a regular taxi that was waiting for us. Surely Alicia had wanted to surprise me, for when I went to give the driver my suitcase, she warned me:

"This is my friend Rodrigo. He's a writer, from Costa Rica. Ever since I found out he drives a taxi, I don't use anybody else. When he's on duty, of course. If he isn't, I'd rather he write. He's very good."

"Here everybody makes a living however they can," he added, smiling. He was tall and thin, and neither his manners nor his appearance were anything like those of the taxi drivers I was used to in Madrid.

Alicia sat in the backseat with me but kept the window between the front seat and the back open and spent the whole way competing with Rodrigo over who could thresh out more things for me to see in the city. Although Alicia had warned me about the cold, I was not prepared for its intensity and, frozen stiff yet captivated by what I was seeing through the window, I barely paid attention to them either on the snowy highway on the way to Manhattan or when we finally crossed the Williamsburg Bridge. Five years since John Lennon's death, Ronald Reagan was still president, and I could not remember seeing so much color in any city I had ever visited: color in people's clothes, on store signs, in the ubiquitous flag . . . When we finally stopped, Alicia expected Rodrigo to join us.

"Just for a while. Turn on the meter and I'll pay you as if for a ride."

Rodrigo laughed at the idea but insisted that he had to take the car to the garage, and he left after we agreed to meet the following day.

"He probably has other plans," Alicia explained to me. We had entered the door to the building and were waiting for what looked like a freight elevator. "He doesn't like Guillermo's friends, he calls them *los celebrities*. He thinks they're snobs. And he's right, I guess."

"Are they famous?" I asked a moment later, just to say something, intimidated suddenly by the new tone she was using with me, as if I were a friend rather than her younger cousin.

"No, absolutely not," she laughed. "He's being ironic calling them celebrities. He says it because some of them give themselves airs. Especially those he doesn't like . . . "

Now she was the one trying to be ironic. We had reached a rectangular landing with two doors. The *loft*, as it was called, that appeared before me when Alicia opened one of them deserved without reservations to be called spectacular: more than two thousand diaphanous square feet of living room and kitchen space, and a second floor, above half that space, and as far as I could see, also diaphanous. The highest part of the ceiling was at least twenty-five feet, and the largest of the many paintings covering the walls seemed custom-made for these dimensions. In contrast, the space was sparsely furnished. There were a couple of armchairs, some bookshelves, two or three sofas, and a dining room table already set for dinner. Guillermo was in the kitchen with two Chinese men in black uniforms—the employees of the catering service.

"There won't be many of us," Alicia informed me, "though more people might show up later for a drink."

At that moment, Guillermo came over to us and gave me a hug that was almost as warm as the one Alicia had given me at the airport. I hadn't seen him, as I had her, since he had left Madrid, and it took me a few moments to update the image of him I had retained in my memory. I found him thin, his facial features slightly hardened, and, above all, dressed with a patent self-consciousness—excessively dapper—that I did not remember being so pronounced.

"We are going to do everything possible to make sure you enjoy your time here," he told me. And then, when he saw Alicia walking over to one of the waiters, he added to her, "Darling, don't worry about anything. Just make yourself beautiful. I have everything under control."

The first guest arrived half an hour later, and the others came ten minutes after that; six in all, if I remember correctly: an Englishman who puffed on long, skinny cigarettes through a marble holder, and who apparently was the boss, in New York, of the Italian division of Sotheby's or Christie's; an editor of *Vanity Fair*, a woman named Cohen, attired in a two-piece suit and looking like a feminist intellectual from between the two world wars; a professor of psychology at New York University who did not stop taking pictures of us with a Polaroid camera; a sculptor, older and very tanned, who had lived in Ibiza and Capri; and a couple who looked deliberately androgynous, possibly even fraternal. I think she was a clothes designer and he a photographer.

As was only natural, I was shy and withdrawn during the meal, in part because I was not yet used to hearing English. Before sitting down, I was afraid Alicia would make an effort to include me, but except for her frequent knowing glances, she managed to let me remain comfortably in the background. She herself, in spite of the fact that her guests included her as much as Guillermo in their conversation, did not participate very much. I think we both breathed a sigh of relief when the bell rang again. We had already left the table and were sitting on a sofa.

"Your friends have arrived," Guillermo said to her in Spanish.

"Your cousin has a truly remarkable collection of friends," he added to me. "All extremely brilliant, though somewhat dissolute."

"Your friends are, too," she corrected him.

"Yes, but you are the star."

I did not perceive any reproach in Guillermo's tone. He was trying to make a good impression on me by teasing Alicia, and there was no question about the smile she gave him in return when she got up to answer the door.

The newcomer was a Spanish painter, Guillermo's namesake, whom they called, to distinguish them, Guillermo el Sevillano. He greeted everybody as a group, held out his hand to me—saying that he already knew that I was Alicia's cousin—and gave Guillermo a hug.

"Why didn't you come to eat?" he asked, ending the embrace.

"You know I can't stay long in one place. I've just come from Brooklyn, and I'm afraid I'm planning on stealing your wife, as usual."

Guillermo laughed, and Alicia proclaimed that she would go out with him only if I accompanied them. I knew she was speaking in earnest because I saw she had stood talking with the new Guillermo for a few moments next to the door before bringing him back to where we were sitting.

"It's Christmas Eve, so the Irish pubs are definitely closed," she announced after we'd left. "We'll have to go to a club."

We ended up going to three, the last one I think was Studio 54, and I soon lost track of the people Alicia introduced me to. If it were not for the long agenda of tourism she had planned for the following day, we would have continued. As it was, we arrived home after five in the morning. I had still not fallen asleep in the bed Alicia made up for me on one of the sofas when the front door opened and I saw Guillermo's shadow climbing the stairs to the second floor. It struck me as odd, for I thought he was at home, but I soon fell asleep. Then I had one of those dreams in which you are partially aware that you are dreaming. Irritated and disturbed by a low and sharp repetitive noise, I thought it was a fan and wanted to get up and turn it off, but I remember telling myself, still half asleep: *What nonsense, it's impossible, it's December and I am in New York. It must be someone crying.*

The next morning I did not see Guillermo. Alicia, already dressed, woke me up and explained that he wasn't feeling well and that we would meet up with him in the afternoon. I suggested she stay home with him, but she didn't want to. *Are you nuts? Leave you on your own your first day in New York?* She was so resolute that I did not insist. We ate breakfast out and after finding both the Guggenheim and the Whitney closed, we didn't bother trying other museums. We walked down a stretch of Fifth Avenue, often having to go around impassive doormen rushing to open taxi doors or returning from them escorting old ladies weighed down with jewels, then crossed Central Park, stopped in front of the Dakota, watched the skaters doing pirouettes at Rockefeller Center, and ended up taking the subway to Chinatown, where Alicia thought it would be easier to find a good restaurant that was open. From there she called Guillermo. I watched her insert the coin in the slot, dial, lean back against the wall, cover one ear, and speak slowly and with concentration; I watched her listen, calm a fear that nobody would have said was holding her in its grip, smile without knowing she was smiling; I watched her straighten up, pull away from the wall, calmly say good-bye, hang up, leave her hand on the earpiece and get lost in her thoughts; then I saw her pull herself together and dial again, as if she were now a different person and in a bit of a rush, like someone who jumps up and dives into the water on a hot afternoon.

"Guillermo's not coming," she said when she returned. "He feels better, but he has things to do . . . I've called a friend who lives nearby. She's half Vietnamese, half Cuban. Interesting mix, don't you think? Her father was in Vietnam at the beginning of the war, a medic with the Vietcong. Then he deserted, or went over to the other side, and brought her with him. She never forgave him because he separated her from her mother, and then he wasn't exactly a very good father. She's very intelligent, but very reclusive. Too much so. I try to get her to go out and have fun. I've introduced her to all my friends, but it's hopeless. Maybe things will go better with you. Do you think you'll like her?"

Alicia put down the menu, which she had been leafing through distractedly, looked at me, and before I had a chance to recover from my confusion, she laughed, as if at herself, aware that I probably was feeling rather ill at ease.

"Forgive me, how silly. I can't stand unhappiness, and sometimes I'm tempted to fix other people's lives. Now that I think about it, she wouldn't be good for you. She's wounded, and you should keep away from people like that. Take my advice. No matter how hard it is or how in love you are, at the first inkling that someone has problems, vanish."

That afternoon, after leaving her friend at the door of the restaurant, Alicia stopped at the first phone booth we passed. Again I saw her cover her other ear, look down at the ground, and speak and listen solicitously. This time, however, after hanging up she did not get lost in thought nor did she stay to make another phone call; instead she came out and announced that Guillermo was waiting for us at the Algonquin Hotel's Blue Bar. *Dorothy Parker's favorite bar. Have you read her?* Then she looked at her watch and considered whether to take a taxi, but she decided we would walk.

Guillermo was waiting for us at the bar. He had his back to us and was talking to the man sitting on his right. He was dressed with the same exaggerated care as the night before. It seemed to me that Alicia slowed down, as if doubting if she should approach, but at that very moment Guillermo turned and saw us.

"I brought the car," he announced. "I thought maybe we'd go out of Manhattan for dinner. Do you remember that restaurant we went to in East Hampton?"

Alicia protested weakly, contending that we had spent the whole day out of the house and that neither she nor I was dressed appropriately, but Guillermo insisted:

"I'll take you home, you can have a quick shower, and then we'll go. It's an hour and a half's drive."

Just then, the man Guillermo was talking to when we entered turned and told us he did not advise it.

"It's been snowing a lot there," he explained. "The roads are probably bad."

I saw that the news upset Guillermo, and Alicia showed signs of sympathetic despondency.

"Let's try if you really want," she offered.

Guillermo, who caught the drift, spoke as if to himself without looking at us.

"No, it doesn't make any sense. I've spoiled your afternoon."

"What nonsense," Alicia replied. "We'll have a drink here, then we'll go eat dinner somewhere . . . In Brooklyn! We'll drive across the bridge and see the lights of Manhattan."

"Did Alicia tell you that this hotel gives a significant discount to writers?"

For a while, it seemed as if Guillermo was overcoming his disappointment and allowing himself to get caught up in Alicia's plans, but after we'd finished our dry martinis, he decided to go home. *I don't feel well. You two go on ahead.* Alicia got up after him and whispered something in his ear. Guillermo shook his head and said good-bye to me with a laconic *Look after her, I don't deserve her.* Surprised and worried, I suggested to Alicia that we accompany him, but she didn't want to. *Better not. He's going through a rough patch. I don't want you to get the idea that he's always like this.*

That night Alicia and I ended up dining at the home of one of her friends. Although she did not show it, I think that she, like me, had not stopped thinking about Guillermo. We returned home early, without stopping at any bars, but Guillermo wasn't there, which I learned only when the front door woke me up and I saw him entering on tiptoe, like the night before.

For the next twelve days, until I left New York, I found more and more occasions to feel bewildered. Nothing significant happened between Alicia and Guillermo in those remaining days, nothing different from what I had observed during the first; until the very moment of my departure, however, I could not shake the sensation that something revealing would finally occur. I spent most of my time with Alicia, submitting to her dizzying rhythm. She refused to exempt herself from even the most conventional tourist rituals, never leaving me for a moment to my own devices; alone or in the company of one of her innumerable friends, she took me everywhere and showed me things I would have been hard put to discover on my own; she was the best hostess one could ever imagine. Also Guillermo, in spite of his mood swings, did everything he could to make my stay agreeable and rewarding. But why that odd dance of approaches and retreats? Why Alicia's air of such disillusioned melancholy? Why her unquenchable thirst for distraction? I left New York with a similar sensation as when I read a text that fails to offer up all its meaning in one reading: confident at having all the pieces of a puzzle but not having found the guiding principle to assemble it. I had been watching a two-week-long hermetic performance, and now I would have to return home and pick up the script in order to decipher it. As it turned out, where I was going I had no script, and even if I did, I would have done everything possible to avoid the task. The piece I'd seen had made me more apprehensive than intrigued, and I had persuaded myself that beyond the ephemeral pleasure of exegesis, what it hid was neither sufficiently edifying nor meaningful to nonchalantly take on the task it bequeathed.

For a few months after I returned to Madrid, I again received letters and postcards from Alicia. Again they seemed hurried, written along with many others, only now she barely mentioned the city and they contained no literary references. The setting appeared between the lines, through the events she recounted. Alicia chose postcards without any recognizable criteria and wrote her letters on all kinds of paper, as if they were composed on a whim and she wanted to put them in the mail before she had any regrets; sometimes she did not even place them in an envelope, merely folding the paper and sealing it with a drop of glue. Some were brief, with flippant descriptions of something trivial she had done or was planning to do. For example: *I got up early today and went out. Too bad you're not here.* Or this: *I have plans tonight with Rodrigo and your Vietnamese girlfriend. I'll send your regards.* They were made up of meaningless fragments of her life in which she rarely alluded to Guillermo. None was significant in itself, even if the metatext they construed let me know that her life had not changed. I believe Alicia was well aware that this would be my conclusion and that in a certain way she took pleasure in fostering it. I could not hope to be taken into her confidence, so this was her way of asserting what she knew I knew. As if she were saying: *What you saw is what there is.* One indication of this was the dissatisfied irony with which, on occasion, she referred to herself with subtly self-deprecating comments: *I've been so terribly busy lately, I just had to take a break.* It's unlikely that she shared this cryptic mode of communication with anybody else, definitely not with her parents or siblings. I suppose that she needed this reservoir of reality, however small and veiled, and that she chose me as her confidant in honor of our old complicity. And, aware of my desire to become a writer, she also probably did so with a certain pedagogical purpose. What she never did was speak directly about the problems between her and Guillermo.

I don't remember who abandoned whom first; our correspondence did not last even a year. I do remember that I was not sorry when it stopped. For some time already I had not understood Alicia's stubborn insistence on remaining attached to a life that so obviously did not satisfy her, and I lost patience with her lack of decisiveness. I thought that, as she seemed destined to leave Guillermo, any delay was stupid. Clearly, I underestimated her.

Years passed, during which I had to reconcile myself to the idea that the anticipated rupture was not going to take place. They continued to come to Madrid every once in a while, but we didn't see each other. This was due in part to the fact that I had managed to publish my first book and had consequently embarked on a convenient career as a fellowship recipient that took me abroad for long stretches of time; in part to the demise of our grandparents' generation, which made contact among the different branches of the family less frequent; and in part to our simply having lost the habit. Once again I had to get used to hearing about them through third parties, and although it pained me to share, in part, my family's views, the truth is that the news I heard was not good nor did it bode well for the future. They had not had children, and now that their phantasmagorical projects had been neglected through the sterile passage of time and their excuses had become utterly futile, they had fallen into an existence ruled exclusively by their whims, without pretense or any will to mend their ways. It had, of course, been some time since anyone thought of Guillermo, in spite of his money, as the good match he had once seemed; but even Alicia, whom the macho conservatism of the family exonerated from all responsibility because of her supposed obligation to follow her husband's lead, was being called to account by the flip side of this same conservatism, according to which the feminine character manages, from the shadows and along circuitous pathways, to make others bend to her own wishes. The main proof of Alicia's failure, beyond her obvious complacency, was her inexplicable refusal to allow other members of the family to benefit from Guillermo's fortune. This reproach, though never stated explicitly, was behind the indifference with which even her siblings began to speak about her, or even worse, to not speak about her at all. Nobody expected anything either from Guillermo or Alicia, their opinions were not required to resolve any family disputes, and their visits to Madrid were no longer eagerly awaited—except by Alicia's parents—as they once had been. Nobody thought that Alicia would be able to act out of noble intentions. Nobody considered the possibility that the anomaly could be even greater than it seemed. Nobody noticed that Guillermo and Alicia, dissatisfied and unhappy, were attempting many solutions, though all were destined to failure. In 1991 they left New York and went to live in Berlin, drawn there like many others by the cultural renaissance set off by the fall of the Wall; in 1995 they left Berlin and moved to London; and in 1997, sick and tired of English "insularity," as they called it, they left London and spent two years traveling in Southeast Asia (Shanghai, Singapore, Hong Kong, Tokyo) until, upon their return to Europe, they settled in Italy—first in Rome, then in a villa near Arezzo. I imagine that in all these places they led their daily lives much as they had in New York. Alicia would have no difficulty making a group of friends sufficiently broad to assure her amusement, and Guillermo would let himself be seduced by the evanescent possibilities that arose from a life wherein he could construct at each moment the idea of himself that appealed to him. How their relationship evolved, in the meantime, is something I don't know and can only presume.

I did not see Alicia again until the spring of 2005, at her father's funeral. She told me they had left Tuscany so that they could be with him during his final illness, and for this reason she had been dividing her time in the past few months between their apartment in Madrid and a country house in the mountains of Toledo, where Guillermo was waiting for her.

"He couldn't come," she explained with a half-hearted emphasis that worried me.

"Is something wrong?"

Alicia responded with a look of assent and said, "This time it's for real. Why don't you come for a few days? Seeing you will cheer him up. It's been many years, but we've been following you from a distance. We've read your books. I'm very proud of you."

I went that same week. Alicia drove me there. It was the first time I had seen her drive and I told her as much.

"I got used to it in Berlin," she answered. "It's such a big city, and there are so many beautiful excursions to go on . . . Then in Tuscany it was very useful; otherwise we would have been too isolated. And now, of course."

"Are you going to stay?"

"Yes, our nomadic life has come to an end. Guillermo needs to live in the country. He's most comfortable there in his present condition, and now that my mother is alone, I don't want to be far away from her. Guillermo would prefer to buy a house in La Vera or in the Sierra de Aracena, but you'll see, it isn't bad here. There's a lot of space, and you don't feel the pressures of urban life as in other parts of Toledo."

"Well, knowing the two of you, we'll see how long you'll last."

"No, really. It's too late for everything," she asserted, with an icy frankness she immediately tried to set right. "You'll see, it's very convenient for what we need."

Alicia was now fifty, nineteen years older than when I visited her in her loft in New York, twenty-five more than when she left Madrid with Guillermo Cunningham. It is superfluous to say that she had aged. She was not the same, nor could she be. However, she was exactly as I remembered her, and exactly how I had imagined she would be before I saw her again. What I mean is that time had not made her irreconcilable with or a caricature of what she had been; she had not gained weight or gotten uglier; she had not become vulgar or changed her style. She had simply gotten older, nothing more. Besides the few wrinkles around her mouth and eyes, and her skin being less luminous, the years had simply made her smaller. It wasn't that she had shrunk—she was too young for that. The effect was not entirely physical. Her gestures and her way of talking were more contained and hence gave the impression that everything in her had been condensed, compressed.

Apart from a certain constraint occasioned by her silences and a lassitude in her linking of one word to the next, her way of relating to me did not reflect any passage of time. She asked me about my books and my life as if we had only recently parted. I did perceive, and it worried me, that along with any sense of humor, which would have seemed out of place, no trace was left of her flirtatiousness of old.

Their estate was quite isolated. We drove along a dirt road and reached a small valley dotted with half a dozen large brick houses separated from one another by an extensive terraced landscape of olive groves and holm oaks.

"You will find the way we live odd," Alicia warned me as we drove down the road, flanked on both sides by elm trees. "We have two houses: the main one, the original manor house, and a smaller one, which was built in the nineteenth century as a guest house. Guillermo lives in the large one and I in the small. In addition," she added hurriedly, as if wanting to leave behind this spatial divorce she had felt obliged to prepare me for, "we have remodeled an old barn. The family that works for us lives in the back, and in the front we have a separate room, almost a small apartment, where you will be staying."

Alicia took me to my room, which was, indeed, much more than I needed. In addition to the sleeping area, which included the bathroom, and a work area with a large table and a picture window almost as expansive as the view it looked upon, it had a large living room area and an American-style kitchen. After showing me the garden (lawn, olive trees, beds of lilies and carnations) and the terrace with a swimming pool overlooking the valley, we went to her house, which looked rather conventional, with a covered interior patio and two floors divided into symmetrical pairs of sparsely furnished and even more sparsely decorated rooms.

"If you feel like it, you can go see Guillermo," she said as we left. As I remained silent, she pointed to the main house and added, "You'll find him on the second floor. He's waiting for you. We'll see each other later."

Guillermo's house was the opposite of Alicia's. Past the entrance hall, decorated with paintings from several eras, rose a staircase that led to the second floor and a series of rooms packed with antique objects and furnishings chosen without any thought to function. In the last of these rooms I found Guillermo, and as soon as I saw him, I understood the grave tone with which Alicia had spoken about him at her father's funeral. He was waiting for me in what appeared to be the library (on one side, Chippendale-style shelves filled with leather-bound volumes, and on the other, Italianate marble shelves with thick art books). He was sitting on a black Chesterfield sofa dressed in a raw linen suit, and the contrast between his extreme thinness and the volume of the sofa and the multicolored density of his surroundings made me for a moment think of a featherless bird.

I stayed with Guillermo the rest of the afternoon, waiting for Alicia's arrival with the premonitory conviction that she wouldn't come, that this strange way of life she had alluded to as we drove onto the property referred not only to a spatial divorce but also to a much more unsettling one. Just like Alicia, Guillermo asked about my books, spoke about the past, his travels, the houses they had had, but he neither mentioned her nor seemed concerned about her absence. Once I'd come to terms with the situation, I wondered, perplexed, what I should do, how I should behave: move freely between the two worlds according to my own whims, or respect the rules I did not know, waiting to be told what to do next? I was about to overcome my qualms and put the question to Guillermo when a servant, one I had not seen until that moment, came to my aid.

"Where will dinner be tonight, sir?"

"At my wife's," Guillermo answered, curtly.

For a moment, I thought the question and the answer included Guillermo, and I had the fleeting hope that I had reached certain conclusions too precipitously. It was Guillermo, after waiting for her to leave, who dispelled the illusion.

"You should go to Alicia. She's waiting for you."

Out of respect for his condition, I obeyed without question, a consideration I did not plan to show Alicia. I said good-bye with a mere "see you tomorrow" and, on the way to the staircase leading to the first floor, took the liberty of pausing repeatedly, dazed by the succession of chests, consoles, mirrors, Roman marbles, African masks, Chinese jars, divans, desks, bureaus, and trunks and shelves and glass cases that in turn contained a multifarious collection of Russian icons, pre-Colombian pottery, Greek vessels, Japanese prints, religious sculptures, art deco figurines, marble miniatures, watches, feathers, votive offerings . . .

I found Alicia in the living room of her house, sitting at a table set for two.

"Explain it to me," I said as I sat down.

I was somewhat rude and abrupt, but she seemed to be expecting it, for she answered immediately.

"There's not much to explain. I assure you we are in tacit agreement. It's the best for both of us; nobody is the loser."

"You never see each other?"

"No, not if we can help it."

"But there must be things you need to do together . . . "

"No, nothing. The servants do everything. Someday I might have to go somewhere with him, but that hasn't happened yet."

"You must cross paths once in a while."

"Sometimes it's inevitable, you're right, but we make sure we each have our own space. He goes for walks in the part of the garden you've seen, and I usually go farther away, to the lower oak grove."

"And the pool?" I asked without thinking, reluctant to believe what I was hearing. "I assume you both use it."

"We try to go at different times. And if not, he stays in one area and I in the other. In any case, as you can imagine, he almost never goes."

"But you have to talk, make decisions together."

"We do so through the servants; we send messages to each other."

"And what if you have to discuss something about them?"

I thought I had put Alicia on the spot, but this was the only moment she cracked a smile.

"We use code. We don't even have to agree on it. For example, if I get a message saying that Guillermo has received a call from his brother telling him he has no money, I know that what he wants, for whatever reason, is to give them a bonus. It's safer than notes, which can always be read."

"But this is madness!" I exclaimed.

"The madness is having stayed together for so long," Alicia answered, "having destroyed each other's lives."

Her tone was so emphatic, her words so devastating, that I was unable to offer an appropriate response. I was on the verge of asking about Guillermo's diagnosis, but I held back. We began to eat and for a while nothing could be heard but the sound of cutlery. As if she could hear my thoughts, Alicia finally broke the silence.

"What I have been telling you is independent of his illness," she said. "Guillermo has been sick for a long time. We've had a long road to travel. We are at the end."

"Is that definite?"

"Absolutely. It's a matter of months. But I don't want to talk . . . It breaks my heart. Guillermo has been my entire life. I have grown up by his side and I love him more than I love my own family. . ." Alicia's eyes grew moist. "It's nothing, don't worry," she asserted, emphatically, when she saw I was about to get up. "I can't help it, forgive me."

"But if it is so serious, wouldn't it be better . . . ?"

She did not let me finish. She had brought the napkin to her face and was drying her eyes.

"Yes, I know. You think we should declare a truce."

I didn't answer.

"Not only would it not help, it would make things worse for both of us. His approaching death does not temper everything that has led us here. It's not easy, I can assure you. We live like this because it is the only way to avoid hurting each other. As I told you, it's the result of a tacit agreement. One could even say that it was Guillermo who pushed for it."

"But what is the problem?" I dared to ask.

"The problem?" Alicia seemed surprised. "It would be easy to blame Guillermo, but that would be unfair. The problem is both of us, what we have done with our lives. Guillermo is a weak person, as you know; capricious, vulnerable, who has fantasized about doing great things and hasn't done a single one; with a tendency toward depression . . . " She paused and looked at me, I don't know if whether to be sure I was following her or because she was doubting whether to continue. "And there's a part of him that he doesn't share with me, that he doesn't even accept and that makes him feel terribly guilty. At first he suffered from bouts of anxiety, nothing he couldn't overcome, but as time passed and his dissatisfaction grew, they became more constant. Sometimes he would stay in bed for weeks obsessively repeating that he had destroyed my life. I also suffered, thinking that I was destroying his. I was brought up to be a complacent wife, to live without asking too many questions, and for years that is what I tried to do. I lacked resolve. I didn't know how to help him. It even took me a long time to realize that I wasn't in love with him. By the time I did, it was already too late."

"But when did it all begin? This way of life, I mean."

"A long time ago. It was already like this a little when you were in New York. But more systematically when we were in Tuscany. That's why we moved there. In a city, in an apartment, it would have been impossible."

"There was nothing that set it off?"

"Nothing in particular. One day, Guillermo again started repeating how he had destroyed my life, and I simply did not have enough conviction to deny it. The veil dropped and, from then on, when it became obvious that I was incapable of offering him relief from his main fear, a constant and paralyzing fear, that was devouring him, he couldn't stand to see me every day—it would have been torture—nor could I stand for my presence to exacerbate his suffering."

"Wouldn't it have been easier to separate?" I asked, then wished I hadn't the moment the words came out.

Alicia placed the fork down on her plate, and her face showed a certain displeasure.

"Yes, I already told you. That is what we should have done. But time passed. We let it pass and suddenly it was too late. That's how life is. Often we don't do what we should and by the time we want to set things right, it's no longer possible. What's best for today has no reason to be best for next year. Circumstances change, and we become weaker or stronger along with them. You'll see, maybe you haven't understood: this arrangement that seems so insipid, which it undoubtedly is, is not an arrangement for us to separate. It is an arrangement that allows us to continue living together. Neither he nor I would know how to live without having the other close by."

Alicia stopped talking when she saw the servant entering with the main course, and as soon as she stopped, I knew she would not start again after the servant left. She had already said everything she had to say. She'd satisfied my curiosity, opening a door onto her private sphere, but the ones she had kept closed, deeming them unnecessary for my understanding of what she had called her arrangement with Guillermo, would remain closed. While we were talking, I was constantly aware of these boundaries, and I avoided, out of fear of interrupting her, asking for details about which she had remained laconic. The unasked questions stayed in my head, and to tell the truth, I intuited the answers. She did not need to answer them; she had told me enough, and she stopped talking because she knew this. They were not relevant, after all. No, they really were not.

I left two days later, though I would return several times in the following months. Upset by the stingy reception of my last novel, I had not written in some time. Without the strength or the incentive to start a new one, I was always looking for excuses to put off the moment of making a decision about my future, and Alicia and Guillermo's house in the mountains of Toledo offered many such moments to me the rest of the spring and part of summer. I usually went—heartened by their hospitality and intrigued, it's only fair to admit, by their strange way of life—when all my prospects in Madrid seemed like an uphill struggle. I wanted to know more, find out if Alicia had been completely honest, and, if she had been, take measure of how far their resistance to each other went, if at some point they would relent. Though I am ashamed to admit it, I also harbored the hope of interceding between them, of becoming their redeeming angel who would hand them a relatively happy ending on a silver platter rather than the dismal one they were condemned to. I was confident that my mere presence, rather than any conversations that would never be encouraged, would achieve this. In spite of the sadness of the situation, I felt comfortable dividing my time between their two universes (lunches with Guillermo, dinners with Alicia), and I think it was reassuring for them to have me as witness to their drama; on one hand my presence lent a semblance of normality, and on the other it offered a safer and more trustworthy means of communication than the servants. Nevertheless, one of the things that most surprised me was how little they used me for this purpose. Rarely was I the bearer of messages, though I was required by each to tell about the other, their moods, what they were doing, and even what they each thought about certain political events. Alicia had good reason to ask about Guillermo, and she interrogated me each time I came from him, but Guillermo's questions were no less frequent. They acted like those neighbors who haven't spoken and have avoided each other for years but enjoy collecting each and every detail about the life of their antagonist, the only difference being that these two did not want to collect news of misfortunes or scandal. On the contrary. What neither of them did in the privacy of our conversations was talk about their peculiar divorce. After my first visit, Alicia never mentioned it again, and till the end Guillermo acted as if my shuttling back and forth between them was the most natural thing in the world.

I must confess that during those days of spring and part of summer, and as opposed to how things had been before, I felt closer to Guillermo than Alicia, and I enjoyed more the time I spent with him than with her. Perhaps the setting had an influence: the welcoming prodigality of his library next to the austerity of Alicia's somewhat icy home; but the fact is that with Guillermo, when we were not ensconced in a comfortable silence, our conversation flowed without pretense or recurrence to preordained subjects and leapt from one subject to another, whereas any silence Alicia and I would get stuck in was thick, or we'd spend our time inanely dissecting daily life, or become bogged down in contrived literary discussions in which she plied me with questions about the books that had been reviewed in the newspapers. I suppose his illness, his awareness of the limited time he had left, lent Guillermo a special kind of serenity, or appetite for forgetfulness, especially propitious for carefree enjoyment, and that without meaning to, Alicia was succumbing, unconsciously, to a sense of urgency to build a future for herself upon the ruins of an unsatisfying past. Be that as it may, and not without pangs of conscience, I found myself at moments missing that innocent but vital Alicia from before she left for America; also not without pangs of conscience, I once in a while found myself wondering if it was really Guillermo who had ruined her.

In fact, I had a hard time believing this to be the case, but lacking any evidence to dismiss that he had, I had no choice but to push away my doubts in order to live in the present exactly as they did. This seemed, after all was said and done, the main goal of their strange pact: to not see each other, to not deal with each other so as to keep the past at bay. As this had nothing to do with me, I had no authority to stir things up.

I would have liked it if they had behaved toward me in the same way, but neither of them reciprocated. This is understandable, I suppose. Whereas they spent their time in seclusion, they saw me coming and going, and they must have felt obliged to ask me about my affairs. They both insisted that I not interrupt my work, either the mercenary jobs I took as a freelance journalist or my literary efforts. It was easy for me to deceive Alicia. If she saw that I had spent the whole day with her or Guillermo, she soon asked me if I felt uncomfortable in my room, if I needed something; all I had to do was shut myself up for a few hours to reassure her and make her satisfied to provide me, along with everything else, literary nourishment during our conversations. She seemed incapable of considering that this solitude, however meager, was not productive. Guillermo, on the contrary, was more demanding; with him it was not enough for me to pretend to be writing. He wanted to know *what* I was writing. At first I dodged him, gave him vague answers, but it wasn't long—partially because of the difficulty of inventing excuses as well as because it pained me to lie to him—before I told him of my paralysis. The cure ended up being worse than the disease. He became so touchingly concerned that from that moment on—his interest disguised as shy sardonic humor—he asked me the same question every time I went up to see him: *Have you started yet?*

In the middle of August, the morning before I was leaving on vacation, he greeted me in a state of great excitement.

"Listen," he said, "I know how to put an end to your crisis. I'm going to hire you to write something for me. I will pay you much more than they paid you for any of your novels."

"That wouldn't be hard," I joked.

"Don't tell me how much. I'll give you four times more than they paid you for your last one. The advantage is that it doesn't have to be a novel. You decide how long to make it."

"The problem is I don't even know what to write."

"That isn't a problem," he answered. "I'll give you the subject: write about me. It shouldn't be too difficult, you already know the end."

Guillermo smiled, but I realized he was speaking in earnest.

"All I ask is that it not be a biography; I won't last long enough and I'm not up to answering questions. I should just be your inspiration."

I told him I'd think about it, and we left it at that; this was the first sign that the end was approaching. To this day I can't understand what possessed him to make such an extravagant proposal to me, if he truly hoped to end my creative drought or if he longed to grasp at a wisp of artistic notoriety that he had so apathetically and fruitlessly pursued his entire life. Perhaps both.

When I returned home from my travels at the end of September, I found several phone messages from Alicia. She did not explain anything, but each sounded more agitated and incoherent than the one before, and I knew, just from listening to them, that Guillermo's health could not be good. I called her that same night and, without beating around the bush, she demanded my presence in the mountains of Toledo. I went two days later, not knowing how long I would stay but equipped, just in case, with warm clothes and the illusive hope that Guillermo's worsening health would at least have brought with it the rapprochement I never stopped hoping for. A very different reality awaited me. Alicia greeted me at her house with two hurried kisses and, after taking personal charge of my luggage, begged me to go see Guillermo without delay.

Guillermo had visibly declined, though not as much on first impression as Alicia's alarm had led me to expect. I found him sitting on the Chesterfield in his library and, if not for his pajamas and the cylinder of oxygen, I would not have noticed a substantial difference from the last time I had seen him in that same spot. But then I did. He noticed me at the door and, whether because his hair was shaved to almost nothing or because when he smiled, the skin on his face grew taut, thereby emphasizing the roundness of his skull, he no longer brought to mind a featherless bird but rather a starving tortoise.

"Finally, you're here," he said. "A bit longer, and you wouldn't have found me alive."

This time he did not ask me if I had begun to write; I was the one to offer the news. I didn't have to lie, for although not extravagantly productive, my time away from Madrid had allowed me to jot down some notes for the first time in months.

"Fantastic," he answered, wearily. "Unfortunately, knowing you, there won't be time for me to read it."

"For your sake I hope that's not the case. You hired me, remember? So you'll have to pay me."

Guillermo seemed surprised, as if he didn't remember our last conversation and his unusual offer, or perhaps he was gauging what wisps of truth my words contained. He answered me, a few moments later, with a prudence that contradicted the timid sparkle that fleetingly crossed his eyes.

"Yes, of course. Speak to Alicia about that when the time comes. How is she, anyway? As you know, without you here the news I receive is as telegraphic as a military communiqué."

I answered that she was worried about him and I allowed myself to add, "You should stop all this. It's ridiculous and it isn't healthy."

Instantly I knew I had gone too far. Guillermo had not expected this, his eyes filled with tears, and he began to cough. I instinctively made a move in the direction of the oxygen tank, but I stopped.

"It's okay, it's okay, I don't need it," he said, lifting one hand as he covered his mouth with the other. "It's over. Let me rest for a while . . . Just one thing," he said, staring at me. "If you accept the job, limit yourself, please, to being a chronicler. Do not interfere. Didn't the narrator in your last novel say that a writer's job is to search through the darkness? Well, do that."

I came up against the same brick wall when I met with Alicia. She was very eager to hear my impressions of Guillermo, but when she found out about my indiscretion, she did not fail to recriminate me.

"You shouldn't have done that. I thought I'd already told you. I beg you, this time do as I say and don't insist with me, either."

I did not try again, no matter how much I longed to on numerous occasions over the following months.

In the meantime, as the days passed in slow monotony, I had to again grow accustomed to being the only bridge between them. I resumed my old routine from the previous summer, eating lunches with Guillermo and dinners with Alicia, though now, due to his weakness, conversations with Guillermo were not as nuanced as before, and our afternoon sessions did not last as long. In any case, I did not spend all my time with them. I shut myself up in my room for hours, at first to read and then, without even realizing it, to write. Moreover, I returned frequently to Madrid, in spite of the fact that I tortured myself over each absence with the thought that I was neglecting them, so dependent, it seemed, they had become on me.

Around the middle of November, Guillermo suddenly took a turn for the worse. For weeks he had refused to take any medicine other than sedatives. He spent many hours dozing off, under the care of two nurses, who during the worst episodes spelled each other at his bedside. Sometimes, in the disorder of his narcotized dreams, he would mistake them for Alicia, becoming angry, muttering unintelligible words, and begging for forgiveness. On one occasion, he opened his eyes and called her by his own name, Guillermo, then began to shout obscenities before breaking down, sobbing like a child.

Fortunately, however, his mind was not always muddled. After his first steep decline, I moved into his house, where we had many conversations, even if they were labored and inconclusive. They seemed like feeble attempts to escape, all fragments of a single conversation that usually began with a question or a statement and often did not require my active participation, though in reality I'm not certain they were not simply thoughts he spoke out loud and would have even if I had not been there.

One afternoon, in order to amuse myself and offer some comfort, I was reading to him some excerpts from Seneca's *Moral Epistles to Lucilius*, when he anxiously interrupted me and asked me if I thought one should pay for the harm one has done unintentionally. Another afternoon, after asking me about Alicia, and as I was searching for a way to respond without bringing to the fore their extravagant divorce, he exclaimed: *Don't worry. It is best. Death is truly a liberation. Tell Alicia for me. We think we are free, but it's a fallacy. Why doesn't anybody tell us that we are not always the same, that it takes time for us to become who we are?*

Even without always understanding what he was trying to tell me, my role revolved around trying, as is only natural, to offer him comfort. A task, in any case, that was not at all easy. On one occasion, for example, while I was wiping his forehead with a washcloth, he grabbed my hand and said he regretted having suffered from such a lack of energy. When I answered that I didn't think he had abstained from many things in his life, he became considerably agitated. *You don't understand*, he told me, *I'm not complaining about only what I haven't been able to do; I'm complaining about what I have allowed myself to do.*

At other times he did not even make an effort to be conciliatory and launched into attacks on Alicia with a viciousness he would quickly regret. *It's horrible what we have done to each other*, he shouted one afternoon. *Why didn't she leave me? It's more her fault than mine. I refuse to carry all the guilt.* More usual, however, was for him to be overcome with anguish. I particularly remember one night when, after hearing the footsteps of one of the nurses, he begged me to lock the door before she reached it. I tried to calm him down, assuring him that he had nothing to fear, but it was futile: *Promise me you won't let her in. Alicia cannot see me like this, now less than ever.*

But as he was reaching the end, after he'd spent an entire week of constant delirium in his sweat-soaked bed, I thought I understood the contradictory feelings his life with Alicia and Alicia herself produced in him. I was watching over his unsettled sleep while reading a book I had picked up at random when I heard him talking to me in a surprisingly lucid voice, one that did not sound like that of a dying man: *What a sad thing life is, and don't tell me otherwise. We believe we have an impregnable interior, a place where we are defended, where we can steel ourselves, but then it turns out that even we can't get in. Even the most elemental things, our dreams, elude our will. How different everything would have been if my desire had obeyed me. Deep down, we have been equals, even in that. In her own way, Alicia and I have been captives of the same incapacity.*

That night, after the nurse on duty relieved me, I went down to see Alicia. I found her waiting for me, as was her custom, in the darkness of the dining room of her house, the only room from which she could see Guillermo's window. It was her way of keeping vigil. By then she no longer trusted anybody but me to judge his state. She had ceased to show any concern about my work, and as a result, except for a few odd moments when I managed to take refuge in my room, I spent the day torn between her constant requests that I spend more time with him and the demand she did not express explicitly, but which I nonetheless felt as an obligation, to accompany her in her distress. We would meet at the end of the day and barely speak. She did not ask me about my conversations with Guillermo. We both knew that we would not have many more vigils to keep, that everything would end very soon, and we did little but let ourselves be overcome by sleep while we waited for the nurse's feared approach. That night, however, I recounted Guillermo's words to her, not so much to comfort her (though this as well), but to give her one last opportunity to offer me her version; I suppose I already felt I owed Guillermo something, and I was on the lookout for the final flourish with which to end the story that I unconsciously was beginning to sketch out. I remember Alicia sitting to one side with her elbow leaning on the table and her forehead resting in her hand, and how she did not change her position. She listened to me without even changing the expression on her face, without even lifting her eyes, and when I finished, she whispered: *Captives, each other's captives.*

One week later, Guillermo died in my presence. I had agreed with Alicia that when it happened I would place a candle in the window and that only a few minutes later would I come down to join her. I did just that. I lit the candle, placed it in the window, turned off the light, left the bedroom, walked slowly past the full bookshelves, crossed the garden, and entered her house, but when I reached the dining room, Alicia was no longer there.

In the depth of the night, the fragile light in Guillermo's window fluttered like a skiff's lantern in the darkness of the sea.

JOANNA

IT IS ODD THAT AT EACH AND EVERY MOMENT LIFE OFFERS US an unspecified number of choices, that we are constantly making choices that change us, taking certain paths and eschewing others, and yet, when we look back, most of us remember ourselves as children much the same as we are today.

I should have realized; there were enough clues to raise suspicions, but it was not until quite recently that I knew.

By the time I was fifteen, my life had already been somewhat more eventful than is usual for someone that age. When I was four, my mother abandoned me and my father to go live with a man in Venezuela, and two years later I witnessed my father die in a car accident from which I miraculously emerged unharmed. For a while I lived with various relatives, then finally ended up in El Escorial, at the home of my maternal grandmother—a strong and affectionate woman who gave me everything she could, but who was shaped by a set of old-fashioned beliefs that view misfortune as a circumstance requiring even more rigorous discipline, not greater tolerance. The misfortune, of course, was mine, orphaned and abandoned as I was, and it was precisely for this reason that my grandmother kept me on such a short leash, lest I forget that life is hard, that there is no respite. To top it off, my grandmother considered the disaster that was my mother, from the unruly and erratic life she had led since adolescence to her inexplicable abandonment of her home just when she seemed to have found her way, to be her personal failure; hence, in whatever ways she had been permissive with her, she was strict with me.

All of which should have made me more worldly than average, not necessarily a cynic full of grudges against the world or a terror to my classmates, but at least one of those boys who seems from a very young age to understand what makes the world go round; one of those boys who get bored in class because they catch on the first time and are always causing trouble but managing to cast the blame elsewhere—inveterately naughty boys who become consummate actors when adults are around, impenitent loafers who surprise everyone with unexpected resourcefulness when required by circumstances. I was nothing like that. I was docile and immature and more introverted than was good for me. My intellectual abilities were judged adequate: I did my homework and passed my classes without problems, but it took some effort. I did not stand out in any way, either for my rebelliousness or for my intelligence, though perhaps I did a little for my physique, quite tall and skinny, and for my apparent fondness for reading and being alone—"apparent" because these activities were pressed upon me by circumstance rather than by any affinity I might have felt.

Winters with my grandmother were excessively monotonous. Winter in El Escorial, as in all summer resorts, was wretched: the population declined and the streets, full of cars and pedestrians during the warm months, turned into a sad and chilly veneer behind which rose ominously the monastery, a fearful shadow that, in spite of being the town's defining feature, its raison d'être, and its origin and main attraction, housed within its walls the school I attended, one of the most dismal I have ever known to exist. Most of my classmates were boarders, and even though I was not, my life did not differ greatly from theirs: the extent of confinement was similar. Unlike the lucky children who attended public schools, I was not allowed to hang out with friends after school or sign up for any extracurricular activities. My grandmother made me come straight home, and I would not go out again. The extent of her inflexibility could not be justified by the cold weather or how early it got dark, for she remained equally strict when the days grew longer and coats and gloves and hats were no longer necessary. It was only from the end of the school year in the middle of June until it started up again in the middle of September that I was allowed a taste of the freedom other children my age enjoyed as a rule. As long as I did not come home late for lunch and was back home by eight, I could wander tirelessly through the streets or venture out into the countryside. Those three months were the only time of year in which my life was truly full. Students tend to consider the academic year as a calendar year; I did the same with the summers, and the result was the same, for like a bear who hibernates until the ice melts, the remaining months did not exist for me—they were lost time.

Joanna. I have talked about myself not because I believe that the information is pertinent to understanding what I plan to tell but rather to better delineate the contrast between us. Starting with her name, and continuing with the straw hat that protected her very white skin from the sun, everything about Joanna was striking and different. Never, not in a hundred years, would we have had the opportunity to meet anywhere except El Escorial in the summer, and even there it could have easily not happened if Joanna, in her feminine and delicate way, had not also been a loner and immature and someone who sought out spots to hide similar to those I frequented. Now perhaps it would be different, but in that era (I'm talking about the beginning of the 1970s), kids our age, and especially girls, still respected the same restrictions on relationships as their parents. We belonged to two worlds destined never to meet: she, to the wealthiest vacationers, those who retained a certain air of the ancien régime in their extravagant habits, and felt entitled to look down on others with more recently acquired fortunes; and I with the stigma of my family history weighing me down—I don't know whose world I belonged to, if not those whom everybody ignored, who didn't fit in even with the gangs of local ne'er-do-wells.

Later I would discover that in her own way, she was also a misfit, an odd fish, but one indication of the distance that I assumed to exist between Joanna and me, and of my reservations and prejudices, is that before we finally met I saw her on two consecutive afternoons in the gardens of the Casita del Príncipe and on both occasions and even though I couldn't take my eyes off her (such was her magnetism), even though we were the only ones there so early in the afternoon, and even though both of us were carrying a book, I fled, feeling like an intruder. And the third time would have been the same if she had not seen me first. It happened at the same time of day in La Herrería, an oak grove where Philip II had had a chair carved into a rock so he could sit and watch the monastery being built. I had nonchalantly taken possession of the royal seat and was absorbed in the pages of a novel when I was startled by a voice behind me.

"What are you reading?"

Joanna was looking at me and smiling, holding a book at her side as if it were a handbag. It was obvious she had had the same idea as me and was amused to find her place occupied by another reader.

"Oh, nothing, a book," I answered, still rattled by the surprise, as two tiny drops of sweat formed at the corners of her mouth.

"I can see that," she said, "but what book?"

At first, her tone of voice made me think that I was not a complete stranger, that she had probably noticed me before, but I soon realized this was not the case. That initial self-confidence, which immediately shortened the distance between us, constituted an essential feature of her personality as much as the timid silence into which she sometimes retreated. Joanna moved between these two extremes. It could almost be said that her self-confidence formed part of her social training, was the rudimentary element of her class position, and the muteness, the fluster that paralyzed her at times, the melancholy, were reflections of the fears she harbored inside. This is not, in fact, a conclusion I reached at that moment nor in the abundance of time we began to share that summer. It occurs to me now, as I make an effort to remember. At the time, I thought those changes mirrored her mood swings. It was not difficult to be led astray in this respect, for Joanna did not behave the same way with everybody. It was with those closest to her, especially her family, that she often became irascible and, without any apparent reason, stopped talking. As she came to trust me more and more, she would take one or another liberty, but until we finally parted I always considered it my fault for having brought up a subject she didn't want to talk about or having done something she interpreted as a betrayal.

Be that as it may, any shadow of unhappiness remained far away that afternoon we met.

The first thing we did was set about the task of getting to know each other. We both liked to read and were confirmed loners, but besides this, an abyss separated us. Whereas I had only ever been in Madrid and El Escorial, Joanna was already a consummate traveler. She was born in Martinique, her French father a native of the island and her mother Spanish; she had lived in New York, and when her parents separated, she had come to live with her mother in Europe, first in Provence, where she had spent two years, and finally in Madrid. She had a brother three years older than her who studied at the Sorbonne, and this is why she traveled frequently with her mother to Paris. She also often went to London, because her mother liked English shops. This was her first summer in Spain, and she did not know if it would be her last. With her mother, she told me, one never knew. The house in El Escorial where they were staying, a mansion with gardens in the aristocratic neighborhood of El Plantel, had belonged to her maternal grandparents, but her mother found it run-down and uncomfortable. She ticked off all these facts without a trace of presumptuousness—if anything, embarrassment—as if her nomadic life weighed heavily on her, and as if the uncertainty of not knowing what her mother's capricious character had in store for her made her uncomfortable. I listened to her with envy, not understanding her distress, and with a certain amount of anticipatory heartbreak, for she forced me to think of her as an ephemeral presence before she actually was. She forced me to acknowledge that one day she would disappear—I had no taste for unexpected disappearances, having suffered too many. I think that therein resided one of the peculiarities of the friendship we were forging: from the beginning we lived each moment knowing it was fleeting. We never had a future. Joanna did not think about it, and I, who would have liked for us to have one, attempted to vaccinate myself against any illusion that would cause me to relive past traumas. The other peculiarity, not so unusual in that era, was how naïve we were. I was absolutely dazzled, bewildered, crazy about her, but it never occurred to me that we could do anything but take walks, sit side by side, and read or talk for hours on end. Sometimes the physical distance between us was so small that a touch or a glance would make us blush; but at other times, carried away by the excitement of being together, Joanna would flirt emphatically. These excesses brought in their wake long bouts of penitential restraint, and I preferred to avoid them. She would become very serious, as if she had done something wrong, and for an interminable stretch I would grow frightened, certain that she was considering not seeing me anymore.

One of our favorite pastimes was to describe houses we would have in the future, flats in the city or country homes, in precise details that were sometimes so preposterous we were obliged to pick up paper and pencil and draw them. In addition, every day we chose one house in town that stood out for some reason, or simply because we liked it, and we played at imagining what it was like inside. Even the least adept fans of psychology would point out that this obsession with houses revealed our unhappiness in our respective family situations and our desire to escape, and surely they would be right, but it seemed to us as natural a pastime as any other, as it also was to enumerate, after our walks, all the people we had come across, describing in detail how they were dressed; or to play a game of catastrophes that consisted of imagining one happening in a specific place—a museum, a zoo, a library, a city, anywhere—and deciding which painting, animal, monument, which book we would rescue first. Thanks to this game I discovered a few things about Joanna that she would probably never have revealed in cold blood, like the day she confessed to me that if a fire broke out in her house, she would save her old nanny, who had been with her since she was in Martinique, before her mother. Now I would be shocked to hear something of the sort, but said by Joanna that summer, with her lily-white skin and that sweetness in her voice and, it was not only acceptable but even natural.

Everything about Joanna seemed natural: what she said, what she did, what she noticed, her slight French accent, the strange words she used. What was unnatural was not being with her. What was unnatural was the life I had left behind and that I would unfortunately have to return to.

Every evening, before separating, we would choose a starting point for our walk the following morning and agree to meet there. We did not need to make arrangements for the afternoon. After lunch, we returned to where we had separated at noon. Joanna's schedule was not as strict as mine, and at the end of the day I was sad to leave her, knowing that it was my fault alone that we could not prolong our time together. On one occasion, I attempted to soften up my grandmother, and thinking that this would make it easier for me to win her over, I asked for permission to eat dinner at Joanna's house. Her response was disheartening.

"What business do you have in the house of people of their caliber? All they'll do is laugh at you. You shouldn't spend so much time with that girl. One must know one's station in life."

I suppose she already knew that on many afternoons, when we grew tired of walking around, Joanna would invite me to her house, and this was her way of letting me know that she knew and did not approve.

Joanna's house had three floors and a mezzanine, where the kitchen and servants' quarters were located. It had a brick facade, and like the entire El Plantel quarter, had been built on the model of Central European villas and around the turn of the century, when it became fashionable for Madrid's upper classes to spend their summers in El Escorial. In one corner of the dining room, which was on the first floor along with two living rooms and a library, was a dumbwaiter that caried the food and dishes to and from the kitchen. The bedrooms were on the second floor, and the third, which had pitched ceilings, was used as a storeroom and a place to hang laundry, and was where Joanna always wanted us to go hide. In general, this was a futile aspiration, for as soon as her mother had gotten word through a servant that we were in the house, she would come looking for us, and with friendly recriminations that Joanna answered curtly, she would make us come downstairs.

Seeing Joanna's mother, interacting with her intermittently as I did more than three days a week, it was difficult to understand her daughter's problem with her. Obviously, I was careful not to share this impression with Joanna. It was bitter enough for her to have to share me with her, sit by and watch the seductive display of attention she lavished upon me and, perhaps even worse, the gratitude I attempted to muster in response. I did not have parents—I barely had any memories of when I did have them—but based on what I had been able to glean from other families around me, I had learned enough about the way adults treated their children and their children's friends for Joanna's mother's familiarity to surprise and flatter me. I assumed that Joanna's blind dismay whenever her mother appeared was due to jealousy, that she wanted to keep me for herself, and the affective schism between them was neither obvious nor dramatic enough to impel me to seek another explanation. At some point I speculated that perhaps she blamed her mother for the divorce, but as Joanna never spoke about her father—as she undoubtedly would have if she missed him—I did not seriously consider it. Naturally, I was too young to know on my own the sinuous intricacies of the human heart, and my world had been too narrow to intuit them or the complex and not always beneficial relationships that kinship establishes. I did not perceive nuances. Things were either black or white because my mother—with her inexplicable departure—had made sure to leave me with this Manichean dualism, and my mother needed only be black for Joanna's mother, by her mere presence, to be white.

How wrong I was, as it turned out.

Joanna's mother was almost an exact replica of Joanna herself with a few extra pounds. She was not obese or fat or even chubby; nature had simply been generous to her by attenuating the difference in their ages with a flattering padding of flesh in areas of her body, such as her face and limbs, that time usually sharpens then ravages. Moreover, she possessed a calm but roguish way of speaking, a graceful slowness of movement, acquired perhaps during her years in the tropics, that seemed like sensuality. At the time my perceptions were not trained to distinguish such things, but I would say that she was a voluptuous woman. I knew from Joanna that she had had children relatively late, so she must have been at least forty-five when I met her, even though today that seems much too old for the image I have retained of her. Needless to say, she compared quite favorably to any of the supposedly younger mothers accompanied by children our age whom Joanna and I came across. The life she led was very different from theirs. According to what I understood, though Joanna could have been exaggerating, she almost always ate lunch out, and almost every evening that I was at her house she was either expecting guests for dinner or preparing to go out to eat. Of this I do have proof, for one of the things that made Joanna most nervous and that most surprised me—literally taking my breath away—was the uncommon frequency with which she exposed herself to us while dressing. I don't mean that she didn't mind if we saw her or even that she would include us in the preliminaries or the final touches, which is not that unusual. I don't mean that she would paint her nails in front of us or gather up her hair then let it fall, fluffing it from her temples with outstretched fingers; or that she would absentmindedly place a few drops of perfume behind her earlobes; or that she would try on different pairs of shoes until she found the ones she wanted; or that she would consult us about how a particular dress looked, or, even, standing in front of the mirror in the living room, that she would assess the fit of her bodice or the height of her neckline as she opened and closed the buttons on her blouse; or that she would run her hands firmly down and over her hips to smooth out her skirt, all without any inhibition whatsoever. She did all these things without a trace of modesty, nonchalantly, so naturally it was disarming, but also—and there I have doubts about the extent of her naturalness and wonder if there was not a touch of exhibitionism—she let us see—or perhaps it would be correct to say, let *me* see, for Joanna was already used to it—things of a much more intimate nature. On one occasion I saw her not so fleeting shadow in the hallway on her way to her dressing room, her blouse inexplicably open and her breasts—the half moon of the aureole of each nipple—peeking out on either side of the opening; another time, a door unnecessarily left ajar allowed me to see her in profile just as she had emerged from the bath, a towel wrapped like a turban around her head, and the one that should have covered her body held between her hands while she dried one leg with her foot resting on the seat of her dressing table. One afternoon, as I was leaving, she came upstairs to say good-bye wearing neither a skirt nor pants, dressed from the waist down in black panties, and not of the opaque variety; another day, in that same getup, she came into the room where Joanna and I were to tell us something, but this time, in addition, she was unwontedly stark naked from the waist up, her crossed arms just barely covering her chest.

Inexplicable, unnecessary, unwonted: words I use cautiously, for I still do not have a clear idea about the modest role I played that summer. Even today, father that I am of two daughters in their twenties, I spend my life in the presence of feminine intimacies much greater than any of those. There is a difference, of course, which is that a father is not perturbed by his daughter's nudity. In the final analysis, I imagine that the determinaning factor is willfulness. When some degree of willfulness plays a part, it is not possible to speak of a simple lack of inhibition. Provocation, then? I sincerely don't know. Why would I think that Joanna's mother would want to provoke Joanna or me? On the other hand, we all know that what makes the world turn is not exactly will. There are habits, passions, commendable goals that prevail through outlandish pathways, genes we cannot imagine that connect us with the most distant past . . . So, as I've said, these visions took my breath away, but I did not judge her. I had no experience. Everything other than my grandmother's sober house and her puritanical customs was unfamiliar to me. Because of my strong aversion to my circumstances, I even tended to consider my life as the anomalous one. I believe I would have looked favorably upon anything Joanna's mother had done.

What if I am mistaken? What if all these words I have been writing are based on an erroneous assumption? What if there is a Joanna somewhere on the planet with children in their twenties, and the portrait I am in the process of painting is in no way faithful? And if I didn't know what I thought I knew? I am entering murky territory, where the lash of doubt stings even more sharply. The worst thing about constructing a story based on a hypothesis is that even when it leads us to a senseless conclusion, we do not toss out all the particulars. The story retreats like an army in defeat but it continues to occupy a place in our consciousness. Even if tomorrow Joanna were to call me and say, I am here in this place on the planet and I still remember you, the Joanna I am giving birth to would not vanish. The real Joanna and the Joanna I have re-created would merge. According to contemporary physics, space and time are one; how vexing that they should be and that the Joanna I knew is now as remote as the one on the other side of the globe who possibly remembers me.

Joanna's brother, whom they had been waiting for since the middle of July, appeared at the beginning of August, after a month and a half of happiness when, each time he was mentioned, I fantasized that he would not come, that something would detain him far from El Escorial until the summer was over. I did not relish the idea of his intrusion. I feared his presence because I intuited that it would bring changes, and my wariness only increased when it was Joanna's mother who announced his arrival one afternoon when Joanna was more withdrawn that usual. In the morning we had climbed Mount Abantos, and in the afternoon, tired from our excursion, our halting conversation, or both, we had ended up watching a movie we'd already seen. When it was over and I accompanied Joanna home, her mother greeted us with exaggerated merriment.

"Did Joanna tell you?"

My face revealed that she had not told me anything, so her mother did. Then she told Joanna that she had canceled a dinner she had planned and that they should rest in order to be beautiful for him when he arrived.

The brother arrived the following day, and I did not see Joanna again until two days later. We had made a date for the next morning, but she didn't show up. That afternoon, though, she did appear at my house—something I had avoided until then and that filled me with anxiety. Perhaps it was the power of suggestion—she was smiling and even ventured a joke as I left her at the door to tell my grandmother I was leaving—but I found her different, withdrawn. That same afternoon, after going for a short walk, I met her brother. I was predisposed not to like him. Without ever having seen him, he intimidated me. Not only was he older but he had already started university, where he was studying law. He had come from Paris driving a car parked on the sidewalk in front of her house, which Joanna pointed out to me. When we were introduced, his behavior confirmed my fears. There was something contemptuous about him, and in spite of my limited experience, I was not insensitive to it. We found him in the summer drawing room, speaking animatedly with Joanna's mother, exchanging jokes, both of them laughing, and when Joanna turned their attention to me, the only thing he said was:

"Oh, hi. So you're the one who's been entertaining my sister."

That was it. Then he turned back to Joanna's mother and the two of them resumed their banter. Later, when he saw that Joanna and I were leaving, he stared at us for a moment, then said to her:

"Don't forget, little sister, I've also come to see you."

I never got used to him, nor he to me most likely, though I must say that my impression of him subsequently improved. His attitude toward me did not cease to be condescending, but at least it was not aggressive; he did not seek out confrontations, and he never made jokes or expressed sarcasm at my expense. He stuck to tolerating me as he would some strange uninvited guest. Perhaps he was so convinced of my insignificance that he did not see me as a rival. If so, he was right.

In my life I have learned that we never thoroughly know a person until we know their family, and that summer with Joanna was when I first observed this. The arrival of her brother (another replica of Joanna and her mother, except with skin not quite as white and a pair of small gray eyes that stared with paralyzing intensity) allowed me to catch a glimpse of emotional geometries I would never have guessed at and see more deeply into others than I had, perhaps, previously intuited but never viewed under sufficient light.

Above all it changed my view of Joanna's mother, to the same extent, I would say, as I ceased to exist for her from the moment her son arrived. It is not that she dismissed me altogether; she was still polite, and though her social life was over, I still enjoyed some unsettling visions of her private domestic moments . . . But she was exultant: all her attention, all her energy was monopolized by her son, and she simply had no time for anything else. Joanna's mother—I can see now—belonged to that class of women who convert maternal love into a yoke and who, in order to hold on to it throughout the different stages of their children's lives, continually and intuitively modify their strategies in order to achieve their irrational goal: that the children never become emotionally emancipated, that the dependence that bonded them to their mothers from birth until they began to be autonomous be perpetuated into their adulthoods. Overprotective mothers, mothers as confidantes, mothers as accomplices, castrating mothers, mothers who aspire to be their children's best friends, wife-mothers . . . The spectrum expands, the masks worn are not always the same, the gradations vary. Nevertheless, in all of them there beats a primitive instinct, something dark and animalistic that connects them with long-gone, prehistoric eras in which families were the group and individuals who were no longer useful needed to forge alliances to guarantee their own survival.

Joanna's mother had not achieved the same level of enmeshment with her son as with her daughter. After all, that type of inter-dependency in relationships, which otherwise cannot be deemed conventional, usually is in one respect: gender roles are maintained. Joanna's mother had completed the process with her son, and with Joanna, she'd gone only halfway—she had partially failed. In spite of Joanna's rebelliousness, however, in spite of her childish tantrums and her silences, her compliance was even greater than her brother's. He seemed bound by the chains of love—always lighter than those of guilt, which bound her. Her mother was so patient, so well-disposed toward her in spite of her insolence, that the invisible faults that Joanna reacted to seemed even more invisible next to her disproportionate response, and as a result, the need to expiate her excesses and even constantly repent strengthened the bond, piling on additional promissory notes for a debt that could never be paid in full because it always grew at the same pace.

One danger of such a psychological analysis, which I have become aware of through years of therapy, is that when attributing certain motivations to the subject being analyzed, the relationship of cause and effect persists even when that subject is acting unconsciously, and without meaning to we assign to him or her a certain amount of responsibility for the consequences of their actions. I never witnessed anything that justified Joanna's attitude. As I remember it, her mother behaved toward her brother like a solicitous lover, and her brother responded like a professional lothario who knows how to offer up appropriate flattery while perhaps already thinking about his next conquest; both, in turn, treated Joanna as someone who functioned on a lower level of understanding, like the child who is frightened by the shouts she hears and bursts into his parents' bedroom, only to find them in a naked embrace. As far as I was concerned, it was all a question of sensations, the perception of a rarefied atmosphere that required a determined person to stand up and open a window. I don't know if Joanna had by then already seen or undergone something else. Her behavior, in any case, appeared to be ruled by a fear so obscure and visceral that it was perhaps only comparable to the power the two of them wielded over her. In their presence she was transfigured, shedding the poise that distinguished her. Nonetheless, there's no doubt that her brother had greater ascendancy over her than her mother. They both, from all appearances, had a harmful effect on her, but he, without much effort, perhaps only a look, managed to bend her will in a way her mother couldn't. This is probably why her mother used him to extend her own power beyond where hers could reach. And the fact is, it worked, in an almost imperceptible way. Whenever we spent time with them, Joanna would leave her house in a daze, as if she had been undergoing enormous stress. It did me no good to try to speed up her recovery by distracting her with questions or forcing her into a conversation about whatever happened to pop into my head. She took her time, barely speaking until the reality awaiting us outside bit by bit began to prevail. Then she would point to a house, make a comment about a book she was reading, or ask me to describe the last person we passed, and we would return to our games as if the dark shroud that had enveloped her had never existed. What else could we do? Did the words exist that could recount her torment? Could I force her to talk when her behavior was beyond my comprehension? I would not even have known what questions to ask. Even if I had tried to push her, it would have been impossible for her to tell me anything. I can assert this wholeheartedly; I know because of my profession, which I will speak about soon, that it is futile to try to get somebody to talk if they are not already willing to do so.

In the meantime, Joanna and I struggled to carry on as we had before, but something indefinable had changed between us. Perhaps this was because in the second half of August, summer vacationers were starting to leave, which reminded me that Joanna would, too, or perhaps I never became accustomed to time no longer being ours, to having to consider, at every turn, the plans Joanna's mother and brother were concocting for us. The small pool in the back garden of Joanna's house, which we had enjoyed almost in solitude, no longer belonged to us as it had before, for now we had to share it with Joanna's brother and her mother, who was no longer satisfied wandering onto the terrace every once in a while to talk to us and now accompanied her son to the pool. One day they took us to the country house of some friends who wanted to see Joanna, and another day, when we were already out on the sidewalk in front of the house, they called to us from the window and asked us to wait for them so they could join us. Every interference, even though not of Joanna's doing, distanced me a little more from her, and this in spite of the fact that there were also happy exceptions, like the day when we were on the way to La Granjilla Park, sitting in the backseat of her brother's car, and in response to his unfortunate and suggestive remarks about the transparency of her dress, she grabbed my hand and did not let go until we had reached our destination.

The end came suddenly, after a morning excursion to some natural pools in the mountains.

The excursion had been Joanna's mother's idea, and at first I was not going to join them because they didn't know if we could return in time to comply with my strict schedule. However, Joanna had made my presence a condition, and spurred on by her adulatory vehemence, I went to my grandmother the night before and obtained permission to miss lunch this one time. I did not, of course, explain my real reason, inventing an excuse that did not include any mention of Joanna. Before leaving, and to make myself more credible, I prepared a sandwich, which I later threw in the trash. Everything was strange from the outset, as if some relentless purpose were pursuing us, spreading painful premonitions along the way. We placed the food baskets in the trunk, Joanna's mother decided to drive, and before I could take my place next to Joanna, her brother had beat me to it. It was a long way, we got lost, and Joanna's mother, who had started out cheerfully singing Creole songs in French, slowly lost her sheen. Once we finally arrived (we had to park the car and continue on foot), she did not hide her disappointment when she saw another family in the spot that she had imagined would be exclusively ours. She wanted us to leave for a lookout point that she know of higher up the mountain, but Joanna's brother had already put on his bathing suit, and, jumping from the rocks into the water, said to her:

"Come on, Mother, relax, don't be so fussy."

I started to take off my pants and my shirt, and by the time I saw that Joanna was not doing the same, it was already too late. At least I didn't dive in; instead I sat with her on a rock, her mother behind us. After a while, tired of swimming by himself, Joanna's brother came out of the water and lay down next to us, his head on Joanna's lap. Her mother, perhaps feeling resentful, hadn't budged.

"Let's eat," she said. "It's about that time, and then we can come back. Maybe we'll be lucky and they'll have left by then."

"At least wait for me to dry off," Joanna's brother answered. "Anyway, they won't stay long. They were just looking at their watches."

"Okay, so somebody bring me my cigarettes. I left them in the car."

I stood up before Joanna, who had to move her brother's head, but her mother stopped me and said I should let Joanna go as she was the only one who was dressed.

I remember everything that followed as if time and our surroundings had expanded.

I saw Joanna's hat disappear back down the path we had come on, and—in part to take advantage of the freedom her absence gave me, and in part out of shyness and in order to put some distance between me and her mother and brother—I slipped into the water at the very moment the other family was beginning to gather up their things. I can't say exactly how long it took Joanna to return, but it was long enough for me to swim across the pond then stand next to some rocks on the other side, frightening a group of tadpoles drawn there by the plankton. I tried to catch them in my cupped hands, but they were slippery and much faster than me, and I managed to snag only one. Joanna's brother came walking around the pond and knelt down next to me.

"It's not even a week old," he said, "its head will get bigger and it'll lose its tail before it grows legs."

The voices of the other family could no longer be heard. Behind me there was a splash followed by an exclamation of delight. Joanna's mother was in the water. Her brother stood up and walked away until he disappeared to one side of the pond behind some trees. I submerged my hands, let the tadpole escape, then turned to start back. I couldn't, though, because Joanna's mother, who had swum toward me, was blocking my way. She touched bottom next to me, and as her upper body was rising out of the water, I felt afraid she was naked. She wasn't. She was holding her arms out at an angle, and with her face lifted, she squeezed out her hair and smoothed it back with her palms. When her hands reached her neck, she lowered her head and the smile adorning her face grew wider; she looked at me and smiled. She then moved one hand toward me and touched my lips with her thumb, as if to wipe them off. I don't know what I was thinking at that moment, perhaps that she was wiping away a drop of sweat or water. The caress lasted an instant—as long as it took her to pull a piece of lichen away from my mouth, which she proudly showed me—but to me it felt like an eternity, perhaps blown out of all proportion by my panic when I saw that Joanna was observing us from the rock where I would have been if her mother had not stood in my way. Her brother reappeared out of the bushes where he had probably gone to pee, and I, now in earnest, began to swim toward Joanna, while her mother, surprised by my quick escape, turned to follow me and saw her daughter.

"Come on, Joanna, don't be such a prude, jump in," I heard her say.

But Joanna, without waiting for us to reach her, had descended from the rock and was walking away down the path. The pack of cigarettes she had gone to fetch was floating in the water.

It wasn't difficult to find her. She was sitting on the ground next to the car. I tried to talk to her but she had wrapped herself in a cloak of hostile silence from which she never emerged, neither at the picnic area where we went to eat after her mother and brother joined us nor during the long way home.

I did not get to say good-bye to Joanna. Two days after the events I have just recounted, and after she had failed to show up for our dates, I went to her house and saw that the blinds were drawn. Only the gardener and one of the servants were there, and they told me that the lady and her children had returned to Madrid. I went home, wrote a long letter, and returned to give it to the servant, asking her to make sure it reached Joanna. She said that she had been hired only for the summer and that once the house was closed up her job was over. Until the end of my vacation, I returned countless times (almost every day, once in the morning and once in the afternoon), and always with the same desultory results: the blinds were still drawn, and the walls, which used to hide such promise, were each day acquiring more of that intangible destitution characteristic of all empty houses. In the fall, when classes began, I returned to my reclusive life, and I could no longer visit with the same frequency. Still hopeful that some weekend or other Joanna and her mother would appear, I acquired the habit of passing by on my way to the bakery on Saturday mornings—one of my few moments of autonomy—and even though I knew that the cold weather made their appearance even more improbable, and that even if I were surprised one day by open blinds, my chance of ever seeing them again was scant, I continued to do so all winter. Then, on one of the first days of spring, I discovered on one of the first-floor balconies something I had not expected and that, in spite of the time that had passed, made me feel ill: a FOR SALE sign. I remembered that at the beginning of our friendship, when she spoke about her nomadic life, Joanna herself had insinuated that this could happen, and I felt like an idiot for having hoped for a different outcome.

I never saw Joanna again, I never again heard her voice, and never, as far as I know, did she look for me. I do know, on the other hand, that she thought about me at least one more time. I heard from her, in a brief and unsatisfactory way, the following year. In the summer, around the anniversary of our first meeting, my grandmother handed me a letter the postman had delivered. It was an unusually small envelope sporting a red stamp with a picture of a man wearing a fez. In spite of the absence of a return address, I had no doubt. I no longer hoped to hear from her, wearily having relegated her memory, together with that of my mother and father, into the memory storehouse where I kept inexplicable things, and I was tempted to tear up the letter without reading it. I was restrained by the look, somewhere between reserved and suspicious, given to me by my grandmother, for whom such an unnecessarily eloquent act would have raised too many suspicions, and by the time I reached my room, my curiosity had gotten the better of me.

My dearest,

I am in Tangier, looking out to sea from the top of the old city, and I feel I can almost see Spain. Have you gone back to read in the seat of the sad king? Do you have a new friend, better than me? I've been alone. I had a friend but he wasn't like you. I don't know if I'll ever return. It depends on my horrible mother. In ten years, on San Juan's Day, will you wait for me at the Casita del Príncipe? Everything was my fault. Forgive me.

Joanna

As I said, the envelope had no return address, so I couldn't answer it. Nor do I know if I would have. We tend to be unfair with loves who have made us suffer, and Joanna's words, in spite of the unfamiliar affection they contained, frightened me. When reading them I felt that irrational contempt that such expressions of sentiment evoke in children or others who lack experience. But more than that, for the first time I started to think (and now I believe this was due only to my resentment) that Joanna was suffering from some kind of mental illness. Otherwise I could not explain the long silence that came before the letter; the broken syntax; the stammering, choppy ideas, so completely contrary to epistolary conventions. She was in Tangier, yes, but, what about before that? Where had she spent the winter? She had had a friend but she had been alone. And what about that date for ten years hence? These questions, and others of a similar nature, hounded me for days along with the unfair conviction, which had shamefully wormed its way inside me, that I had let myself be fooled. Was Joanna a strange, wounded, complicated creature? Had I been drawn to the wrong person? I needed to leave her behind, stop thinking about her.

But I kept the letter. Days passed, months passed, I found new friends to spend time with, and it did not occur to me to throw it away.

Some time later, when Joanna's features had already blurred in my memory, something happened to me purely by chance.

In my last year at school, about two years after having received her letter, I had the arguably good fortune of finding her in an issue of one of those publications that at the time were called "society magazines"—the fashionable ancestors of the current celebrity gossip magazines—that arrived in my hands by chance (probably while waiting for my grandmother in a doctor's waiting room). It was an article about the debutante ball of a young lady from the upper echelons of Madrid society. Among photos of the honoree in full regalia with her parents and representative guests at the party, I found one that immediately made me break out in a sweat. The caption under the photo read: *Miss Joanna Mornes, on her way through Madrid, with the happy debutante.* There was Joanna as I had never seen her, wearing a strapless dress that the article said was of blue velvet, her eyes and lips lightly made-up, and a pearl necklace. She looked older, but so would have I to her. The first thing I noticed, however, was not this, but rather the contrast, which perhaps only I was able to perceive, between the obligatory smile she sported and the sadness in the depths of her eyes.

I cut out the photo and kept it with the letter, and though I never committed the crime of buying one of those magazines, for the longest time thereafter, whenever I came across one in a doctor's waiting room or at the barber's, I would pick it up and flip through the pages, looking for Joanna. The act was automatic, so internalized was my eagerness to know of her. Luck never smiled on me, though it is true that as time passed and the search became more complicated due to the inevitable changes in her appearance, I usually did not have time to look through more than a few pages. At first this was not the case; at first I had only to scan them quickly.

In the meantime, life went on. I attended university, where I pursued an academic career not pursuant of any degree, which consisted of taking introductory classes in a range of different departments. I began in philosophy, not because I had any real vocation but rather influenced by the times (Franco had died and Suárez was struggling to carry out the first reforms); I then switched to psychology, and after a short sojourn at law school, I ended up in philology, which I erroneously thought would nurture my love of reading. I would have continued in the same vein, jumping from one field to another, had my grandmother not died; in any case, she, unlike me, had had all but enough of my inconstancy, and though I inherited her house in El Escorial and could have prolonged my academic dilettantism, I had one of those attacks of conscientiousness that often follow a loss (I had been left alone, without any family), and I decided to get my life on track. My way of doing this, in a totally haphazard fashion, was to take a job in the reference department of a radio station. Three years later, I believe aided by my eclectic education as well as a grave tone of voice that inspires confidence and is pleasant to listen to, I began hosting a nighttime radio show, a call-in program on issues of health that, with some ups and downs and several changes of name and focus (what constitutes "health" has been quite flexible for some time), has been on the air for an incredible thirty years.

Radio has given me everything. Through the radio I met my wife, with whom I have two daughters, and radio has allowed me to live a comfortable life with enough free time to pursue other interests. I still read a lot, and not only novels. As has perhaps shone through some of what I have already written, I increasingly like to read popular science and history. I am interested in the origins of the universe and the beginnings of mankind. I have a reasonably happy life. I began psychoanalysis at the university, when my mother's abandonment and my father's death still weighed heavily upon me, and with long interruptions I have continued till today. I don't think I need it any longer, but it constitutes a path to self-knowledge that would be difficult for me to give up.

I would be lying if I said that in all this time I have never been able to get Joanna out of my head. I have remembered her only occasionally, but in a way that could be called persistent because of its steadiness over the years. The most trivial circumstance could bring her back to me: my daughters at the age she was when I met her, a news item about the French Caribbean, a trip to El Escorial, a visit to a palatial mansion along the Paseo de la Castellana, a mother and daughter passing by me on the street, a movie or a book (I remember one by Jean Rhys, who was born on an island near Martinique, and more recently, some stories by Alice Munro with adolescent girl characters who could well have been her spitting image) . . . Sometimes it was merely a flash that the task at hand, or more pressing thoughts, forced me to leave behind; but at other times, I would delightfully linger, imagining how life might have treated her. I wondered what she might be doing, where she might be living. I assumed she was married and fashionable, settled in a foreign country with a husband who was possibly a diplomat. It's odd, but I never imagined her unhappy; in some strange way, without any news of her and with the insidious precedents that I have described, my subconscious sought benign rather than painful outcomes when it came to finding a place for her imprint in my memory. I think this means that the resentment I initially felt had melted away; I also think this was the expression, on a deeper level, of an exacerbated longing with which I rooted out the latent fear that she would still be wretched.

It never occurred to me to look for her. What sense would that have? I did not even give in to the temptation of making minor inquiries, such as looking for her name in a phone book. It is better that people who separate from us at a particular time return on their own or don't return at all. This is the maxim I have followed with my mother, who may or may not be alive, and it also worked for me with Joanna.

I could have continued in this way if it had not been for a call we received on my radio show, *Looking Out the Window*. It was not Joanna, no. It was a young woman, more or less my daughters' age, or perhaps a bit older. She seemed very well educated, and nervous; the trembling in her voice was a sign that she was embarrassed by what she was doing, not so much because of the possibility that somebody she knew might be listening, which is what most people fear, but because she was listening to herself. She was the kind of person who cannot imagine calling in to a radio show to share a secret with thousands of anonymous listeners, who finds it degrading. Nevertheless, she had done just that, and she did not know where to begin . . .

One digression: the subjects we deal with, as I said, are quite varied, and the listeners who call us do so for many different reasons. One of the most frequent ones is loneliness—people who feel lonely and say so, and many others who are but don't admit it and either invent or exaggerate problems just so they can talk. Then there are the sick, or their family members, who describe their hardships to console themselves or offer consolation to others; or those who have noticed a strange symptom and, before going to the doctor, seek a preliminary diagnosis; or the depressed, or those who suffer from social diseases such as compulsive gambling or alcoholism . . . Another contingent is made up of people who are economically underwater, the unemployed, those with debts, others who scrape by on pensions and miserly salaries, some who have lost their homes or their businesses or are on the verge of doing so. And then there are those who are looking for advice about concrete problems, who are involved in a civil lawsuit or a contested inheritance or who don't know how to get out of an abusive situation (neighbors confronting neighbors, employees exploited by their bosses, divorced couples trapped in aberrant agreements), or those who have been cheated by individuals or by companies who hide behind bureaucracies to avoid responding to their complaints. And, of course, those whose families are hell, who cannot stand their parents or their children, or have discovered they are being betrayed, or they are the ones doing the betraying and have a guilty conscience. And those who are ugly or fat or are stigmatized by it; and those who walk the streets or who have strange or dangerous jobs, or those who suffer from some kind of sexual anomaly, or are lunatics, or are obsessed with politics, or are exhibitionists and provocateurs; and the troublemakers; and the good Samaritans who offer compassion for the misery they have heard . . . It is impossible to classify them all using one set of criteria. The majority belong to what the sociologists call "the middle-middle class," but the spectrum is broader, as much below that bar as above it. Approximately 30 percent are "regulars"—people who like the forum we offer and call in more frequently than we would like—40 percent call occasionally, and the remaining 30 percent never call back. Those in the last category are lonely, worried about something, and they pick up the telephone only that once.

The girl I am describing was one of these, the kind I and my colleagues prefer. They afford greater satisfaction, are more authentic—if one can say that—and are easiest to help precisely because of the unique nature of their call. Some of them, moreover, tell of quite unusual personal predicaments. But one must tread very carefully, know how to deal with them, for rarely do they come right out with their problems. Beset by shame, they reveal only a tiny, often irrelevant slice, and my task consists of pulling on the knot, untangling it tenaciously, always at the risk of them suddenly thinking better of the whole thing and hanging up. One could immediately perceive that this girl was walking a very fine line.

She was calling because she was distressed by something that she did not know if she had seen or only felt. She lived alone and had a long history of conflicts with her father; based on her description, I deduced that he was an egotist and emotionally immature, someone who, in addition to never pursuing anything in his life besides his own satisfaction, had collected an array of children from various marriages, whom he did not take care of at all or only very erratically, and whom he raised on shifting ground, rewarding them or punishing them according to criteria determined solely by the narcissistic fluctuations of his moods. But she had not called to talk about her father's character, which she had accepted, but rather something she had seen him do or that, as I already said, she had sensed that he had done to one of her sisters, who was still a teenager. She was the oldest and for this reason felt responsible for her siblings and looked out for them because she knew what they would be facing. The story she recounted, hesitantly, was long and had ramifications for other members of her father's family; she had only been able to piece it together by collecting fragments here and there, and from the outset, with a terrible sense of guilt. She told me of massages her father gave her when she was a child while sitting astride her, of his erect penis pressing against her naked back when he leaned forward to rub her shoulders. She told me about a sister who refused to see him from one day to the next and was never willing to offer a reason, who could only cry every time she asked her what was wrong. She told me about a younger sister, the reason for her call, whom she discovered sitting naked with him on a couch . . .

When one hears such stories, one must be careful. And not only, as I said before, to avoid an abrupt end to the conversation. One must very quickly determine if what one is hearing is true or false. There are many fantasists who tell murky stories hatched in their imaginations as if they were real, crazy people who cannot distinguish between the slippery insides of their minds and the world outside, and who are eager to spread their nightmares to others. These people should not be encouraged with questions, quite the contrary. They might start ranting. One cannot refuse to listen to them, but one must contain them, carry them along gently to the end of the conversation without making them feel rejected. It is not difficult to tell the difference. In addition to a certain loquacity, they all share a twisted logic that cannot go unnoticed as soon as you pay attention. But speed is essential. It can also be very detrimental to make a mistake and believe that someone who is telling the truth is in fact one of the crazy ones. This would inhibit them, silence the story that they need to share, and cause great harm, stifling, perhaps forever, the words they had wanted to say.

I knew immediately that the young woman who called that night was not making anything up, that she was speaking the truth; her tone conveyed conviction; the words she chose, in spite of her nervousness, were sensible; her assessment of her father had the coherence of meticulous observation and contemplation; she became choked up with emotion where it was appropriate, and she skipped over the superfluous and went deeper into precisely those areas where my own questions would have probed, without any need for me to formulate them. When I said what we are obliged to say in such cases, that she should report it, she had obviously been expecting it.

"I know but I have not seen. Unless my sister speaks out, it will be my word against our father's, and the damage I could cause might be worse. I suppose she is not fully aware of everything, as I wasn't when I was little . . . But if she were forced to testify, it could be traumatic."

There's no point in my lingering over the arguments I gave in my attempts to persuade her, nor in those she presented to me in response; I figure we went back and forth three or four times. Then I gave up. I had not succeeded in making her budge an inch; it even seemed, on the contrary, that she was becoming impatient, and I was afraid I would lose her. I should have left it there—my colleagues in the sound booth were making signs for me to cut, other calls were waiting to be answered—but I decided to hold on, and I asked her about the ramifications for the family members she had mentioned then dropped at the beginning of her story when she shifted the focus elsewhere. She returned to the very close relationship her father had maintained with his own mother, her grandmother, and her suspicion that this had been his initiation into the unnatural habits he had repeated with his daughters, and she spoke about a sister of her father, whom she had never known, but who, according to an old nanny who was still alive in Fort-de-France (Fort-de-France, she explained, was the capital of Martinique), had spent her entire short life trying to escape from him, until one day, on the verge of getting married at eighteen, and hours after discovering her fiancé in her mother's bed, had torn a sheet from that same bed, tied one end to the balcony and the other around her neck, and jumped.

THE LAST COLD FRONT

FROM THE BEGINNING OF 1982 UNTIL SEPTEMBER 1983, WHEN I was fourteen years old, my mother was involved with a Latin American professor who taught at a French university. As we were living in Madrid, they saw each other every two or three weekends and during holidays. Sometimes my mother would visit him in France, but more often it was he who visited her. When he did, he slept at our house, in my mother's room, where there were two beds and where she had tucked, into the corner of a painting hanging on the wall, a photograph of him, smoking—a black-and-white portrait with his face half hidden by his hand that was holding the cigarette.

It was not the first time my mother had had a boyfriend. I think there had been two or three others, one of whom we had lived with for a summer, but I had never given them much thought, or maybe I had been too young to include them in that category or even know what it consisted of. At that time, my father continued to interfere in whatever way he could. As the house we lived in was the same one he had left, he took the liberty—which my mother did not oppose with sufficient effort—to come see me whenever he felt like it, which sometimes led to rather awkward situations.

My father was still coming over to visit when my mother fell in love with the Latin American, but we had moved to a small house to which he had no key, and he himself had settled down a bit more, his love life no longer as chaotic for he was living with a woman. At least now he announced his visits, though they continued to be sporadic and unpredictable.

I think my father could not stand being around my mother, but I also think that he remained in love with her for many years. This is why he hindered, as much as he could, any relationship she had. He did not want to be involved with her, but he also did not want her to make a new life without him. Then he was left without the house as an excuse.

My mother turned forty right around the time the Latin American showed up. She was a tall, good-looking woman who dressed stylishly and whose eloquent elegance was reflected in her excellent posture as well as her way of talking, walking, and moving her hands. All of which garnered her the admiration of men but also lent her an aura of inaccessibility, which she was well aware of and even cultivated with aristocratic aloofness. Her lack of luck in love was in part due to so few men daring to make the first move, in part because of her taste for less than conventional men. She felt an aesthetic attraction to a certain kind of decadent sophistication that led her to focus on specimens so blasé about everything that their lives often lacked any direction at all. I don't mean to say that she was blind to their defects or was scornful of them but that she simply had unequivocal trust in her own ability to set them on a better path.

Then there was me, our very close relationship, the fact that she seemed to subordinate everything to what she considered best for me. The problem was not that she would forgo doing things because of me; she traveled and stayed out late more frequently than other adults I knew. In the long run, what discouraged her suitors was that our relationship was so solid and exclusive that it apparently left no emotional space for another of like intensity. This quality was intangible, disembodied, and when not translated into something concrete, should not have bothered them; it did, however, feed a rivalry with me and awoke dormant feelings of jealousy that at moments of crisis led to impossible demands, which, when not met, poisoned the relationship.

One such demand was that my mother forget about me for a few hours. Another was that she not call me two or three times a day when she was out of town. Yet another was that she take a long trip without me. My father, as I have said, would come to see me, take me out to eat or to a movie, then drop me off at home. He did not take me on vacation or to spend weekends with him. At first this was because he was swallowed up by the egotistical chaos of his reclaimed bachelorhood, and it simply never even occurred to him; later, even if he had wanted to, he lacked the necessary living arrangement; and finally, at the time I am describing, the woman he lived with wouldn't allow it. My mother was the one who suffered most from this state of affairs, for she was never free of me. Everything that happened to me was her responsibility. She went out many nights, and on some weekends she could leave me with the live-in maid, but not for longer stretches. And, of course, when she was gone, she had to manage things from a distance, call me to find out how everything was going.

My mother could never forget about me; neither should she have nor was it possible nor do I think she wanted to. As a result, there always came a point when her boyfriends asked for more: that she break off completely from my father. For she and I both to do so.

The reasoning they gave in somewhat veiled terms was simple enough: my father did not adequately fulfill his paternal role, it was futile to expect him to contribute to my well-being, she could not ask anything of him, so why not do without him altogether? In that case, they suggested, with him out of the way, they could become my adoptive father and the three of us—my mother, he, and I—a perfectly happy family. Without the threat of my father's interference, they would feel capable of taking on responsibilities. They would also then not feel as impinged upon by the lack of freedom, or as importuned by the constant phone calls when they took my mother on trips or by my constant presence.

My mother never agreed. She neither agreed nor, of course, did she tell me about these demands until many years later, when not only the Latin American professor and his predecessors but also any desire of hers to settle down with a man, live once again a harmonious life in a couple were history.

Apart from refusing that I break off from my father, apart from her conviction that my relationship with him might be deficient but was necessary and her trust that things would normalize little by little, my mother's *no* was determined by her own feelings. Returning to live with my father never figured in her calculations, but her affection for him remained intact, and she would never have betrayed him or left him in the lurch. Nor did she ever judge him. He might irritate her or even make her angry, but deep down she considered his deficiencies to be the result of his weak character—of which he was the principal victim—and she forgave him the way one forgives those who are sick or who, though not bad themselves, act in ways that cause bad things to happen.

My father was a good person, and he loved my mother and me, of this we had no doubt. The problem was that he never felt obliged to back up this love with deeds. On one hand, he knew he was loved in return and thought, as a result, that everything would be forgiven; on the other, he had total confidence that my mother would make a success out of me and little in his own ability to deal with the practical aspects of life. He believed he lived in a permanent state of emergency, and if in order to address it he had to forgo his paternal responsibilities, he did so without much remorse and certain that we would understand. The problems he considered urgent—whose solution took precedence over everything else—had always to do with him, not with me. I was covered by my mother.

And so it was. Neither my mother nor I questioned him. We no longer agreed with him, however, that his situation was fragile, or, above all, about the suitability of the remedy with which he pretended to shore things up: his partner at the time. Fifteen years before, taking advantage of the political reforms one could already see on the horizon, he had founded a publishing house that had published, with some success, classic texts of politics and sociology, but with the arrival of the new era he had been incapable of extricating himself from the prolonged binge of euphoria lived out in the country's night spots; the same inconstancy that had fatally damaged his marriage with my mother also affected his work. He wouldn't have been a bad translator—with his curriculum and experience he could have done all kinds of work at many publishing houses that were being started—but, partly due to pride and partly to his paralyzing shyness, he had preferred to hold on to what he considered his life's work, thereby dooming it to a slow and painful death. Just as he was hitting bottom, his girlfriend rescued him from his pernicious lethargy, but as a result he fell into an even more dismal one of a spiritual nature that made him a prisoner of another's will. They scrapped the publishing house, and the little capital they were able to retrieve was invested in a clothing store that belonged to her, not him. He had his upkeep guaranteed—the specter of ruin that had been tormenting him was dissipated—but he was no longer master of his own destiny. His main role was to yield to his girlfriend's plans, which of course never took into account any of my or my mother's needs. The time my father spent with me was, mostly, what he managed to scrape together on the sly.

In those years, 1982 and 1983, when his relationship was still new, the amount of that scraped-together time was still more than it would be later. He would come by the house and take me out to movies and bookstores, and he often invited my mother to join us: stolen moments the three of us spent happily, enhanced by his wonderful sense of humor that never failed him, in spite of everything.

For example, he would tease my mother for sleeping so much,

calling her a bear, and then he would imitate the maid, and with pretend servility, exaggerating the formal way servants used to speak to their employees, he'd ask: Has madam slept well? Would madam like some fresh-squeezed juice? My mother was not always amused by his jokes, but generally she accepted them, knowing that they did not contain any ill will and were his way of establishing an affectionate rapport. He wasn't any more restrained with me. If we were watching television and there were advertisements for dolls or toys that I had not played with in years, he would ask me which I wanted for Christmas and would tell me to waste no time writing a letter to Santa Claus. Nor was the maid exempt from his teasing. He would interrogate her about her boyfriend, whom she went out with on Saturday afternoons and all day Sunday, and tell her that sooner or later he was going to have to speak to her parents about him. Not even my dog escaped: he called him young master Tobi because the concierge of our building, who was like a character out of a Galdós novel, insisted, in spite of our protests, on referring to me as the young master.

Whenever my father was at the house, he acted like a father and almost like a husband, as if he had never left, as if when evening came he was not going to leave for a different house and get into a bed we did not know and continue making jokes, different jokes, I presume, that we would no longer hear.

I now realize that the relationship between them was, deep down, pretty peculiar. The separation wasn't; it was the typical story of a final straw that broke the camel's back. My father became ever more distant without there being any real reason for discord. While carrying on an active night life, he went from occasionally spending a couple of nights at the publishing house to slowly turning this into the norm, as my mother's dismay grew apace. She felt lonely, pushed aside, and even humiliated; she finally managed to disengage from him, something that upset my father only later, when, sunk in chaos, his entire life foundered. The paradox is that he found the shelter my mother was no longer willing to provide him, and out of pride he would never dare ask for, with someone who placed infinitely more restrictions on his freedom than the bare minimum my mother would have made her peace with when their troubles began. At the time I am speaking about, she was not wholly indifferent to this; in fact, it had become a reason to feel insulted in retrospect. Nonetheless, there survived between them a primary affection, a bond, like that between siblings, which survived the assaults of time and their mutual discontent.

My mother's involvement with the Latin American professor did not interfere with this state of affairs. He lived in France, so there were no obstacles to my father visiting us whenever he wished and perpetuating the fiction that he knew nothing about my mother's new relationship. Only with me did he give himself away, like the day he discovered the portrait of him my mother had put up in her bedroom.

"What did you say he teaches?" he asked me, pretending not to know and in order to gain some time to toss an ironic remark my way.

"Literature."

He looked at the books my mother had on her bedside table and picked one up: *Mateo Manso's False Memories* by Joaquín Trafford Iribarri. Disdainfully leafing through the pages, he said:

"Well, if these are the authors he teaches, I feel sorry for his students."

"The author is a friend of his," I said, trying to defend him. "Anyway, he teaches Latin American literature, so he can't very well teach *The Leopard*."

My father thought of himself as a good reader, and he always talked about a novel he would one day write. At other times he'd say he had no talent but that he would make of me the writer he would like to have been. He gave me books by Scott Fitzgerald and Radiguet and Giorgio Bassani and Joseph Roth, books we already had in our library at home but that seemed to me like the best gifts in the world.

My father's sarcasm that day irked me because my relationship with my mother's boyfriend was still good. One could say that my judgment, like hers, was somewhat clouded. His visits to Madrid were usually brief, one week at the most, so there was no time for us to settle into everyday life; we were always on holiday, and our spirits remained high. He and my mother would go out at night to dine with friends, they would return late and wake up smiling, inclined to do little more than while away the time. We frequently ate lunch out and took short trips to cities near Madrid, such as Segovia, El Escorial, or Toledo. My mother's boyfriend also had a hilarious sense of humor that would turn ludicrous as the beer he drank as an aperitif combined with the wine he drank during lunch, the glass he'd have after lunch, and his afternoon whisky. My mother's boyfriend drank a lot, but as we were almost always out, this did not seem so strange.

Almost the entire year of 1982 went by without any significant upheavals. We spent part of the summer with my mother's boyfriend in El Ampurdán, at the home of some friends, and in the fall my mother announced that at the beginning of the next academic year he would come live with us in Madrid. We would sell our house and buy a bigger one, in which I would have my own mini-apartment, where we would put any furniture and paintings that I wanted from our current house that my father had not already taken away. She told my father of our plans. I could tell he didn't like them because he didn't let her finish talking, which is what he always did whenever he was rebuking her, and that afternoon he didn't crack a single joke and he left early. Then, the next time we saw each other alone, he brought it up and questioned, with a mordant wit that bothered me, whether they were really going to give me a room as big as the one they were promising.

"They will, you'll see," I said, cutting him off. "And if we find a house with two doors, I'll have a separate entrance. That way you can keep coming whenever you like."

At that my father stopped expressing his reticence and turned bright red, as he always did when he was touched.

A little more than a month before the end of the year, in November, two things occurred that affected everybody's mood: my father started talking about the new publishing house that he was planning to start with a friend from university who had agreed to be his partner, and I had my first fight with my mother's boyfriend. He arrived one Friday to spend the weekend with her, they went out for dinner, and on Saturday, while I went to the movies with some friends, they stayed home. When I returned around nine, I found them in the living room. I saw a bottle of whisky on the table and noticed that my mother was nervous; obviously not wanting me to join them, she suggested I go straight into the kitchen to make myself something to eat.

"Let him stay," her boyfriend blurted out somewhat harshly.

"He'll eat with us."

I stood there, facing them, waiting for my mother to say something, when suddenly he stood up, came staggering toward me, grabbed me by the shoulders, and after planting a damp kiss on each of my cheeks, he muttered:

"If you don't, I'll never get you to love me more than that failure of a father of yours."

"Don't say that," my mother cut in, firmly.

"It's true," he replied. "A failure and an imbecile."

Although he was still gripping my shoulders, he had turned to look at my mother, and I took that opportunity to push him away; as bad luck would have it, he tripped and fell sideways onto a glass case where we kept the objects my father brought back from his travels; the glass broke and he ended up bewildered, his elbow stuck inside. My mother, who had stood up without my noticing, helped him up and sent me to my room. From there I could hear them arguing. After a while there was a knock on my door, and before opening it I knew it was him, coming to apologize.

It's likely that this scene would never have taken place had my father not, around the same time, begun to fantasize about getting back into publishing. At the time, I did not think to connect the two events, above all because the fight was over that same evening and left almost no trace besides a minor mistrust of my mother's boyfriend, whereas the issue of the new publishing house became a recurrent subject of conversation.

The night of the fight, my mother came to my room a short while after her boyfriend on the pretext of bringing me a sandwich. She entered without knocking and sat at the foot of my bed, where I was lying and pretending to read. I thought she would scold me for pushing him, but she didn't mention it.

"Don't take it seriously," she told me as she patted my leg. "Don't pay any attention to what he said. He's drunk."

"I've already forgiven him."

"I know," she answered. "You are a wonderful son. But I don't want you to hold a grudge. He's a little jealous, that's all. He'd like you to love him as much as you love Papa."

"But that's impossible."

"Of course it's impossible," she smiled. "But there's nothing wrong with him aspiring to it, don't you think? He'll get used to it. Give him time."

The following months were teeming with conflicting incidents, abandoned plans, and others that came to take their place.

Two weeks later, when her boyfriend was not in Madrid, my mother brought up the subject of my father at an Italian restaurant where we often went on Sundays. The previous Friday, not expecting a visit from my father, I had arrived home from school and found the two of them in the living room; although it was obvious that they were talking about something important, they both changed the subject when they saw me. That Sunday at the Italian restaurant, however, after we ordered our food and the waiter had walked away, my mother directly broached the subject.

"Your father has asked me to lend him money to invest in the publishing house he wants to start, and I have told him I can't give him any."

I didn't respond.

"There's nothing I'd like more than for him to start up a new publishing house and for it to be a success. Also, the fact that he has a partner is good news." She paused to give the waiter, who had returned, time to serve us our drinks. Then she turned back to look at me, and, as I still had said nothing, she added, "Say something. What do you think?"

"That if you didn't have a boyfriend, you'd probably give it to him."

My mother shot back a response.

"That's not true. I'm not giving it to him because I don't have it. I'd have to take out a loan, and I don't think it's a good idea that he always turns to me."

"What if he still lived with us?"

My mother looked surprised.

"If he still lived with us, it would be a different story . . . It would mean we were still married, and then I would almost have to. But there's no point in wondering what if. He's living with someone else. He should be asking her for it."

"What if she won't give it to him?"

"If she won't give it to him, I don't know . . . too bad . . . Maybe he should rethink a few things . . . All I know is that he hasn't asked her yet. He admitted that himself on Friday when I explained my decision."

I didn't say anything.

"What I don't want is for you to think I'm acting out of resentment. My duty is to protect myself in order to protect you. Imagine what would happen if the publishing house fails and I have to pay back the loan. It wouldn't be fair, don't you think?"

My mother scrutinized me. I wanted to find a smile on her face but didn't. I picked up the empty wineglass that the waiter had not removed and began to balance it between my fingers.

"I guess," I said.

"In a way, I'm proud that he turns to me," she continued, visibly more relaxed, "because it means that he trusts me, that he knows he can count on me. And it's true, he can. But really, I don't think it's good for him that I'm the one to pull his chestnuts out of the fire yet again. He has to get his act together. He's never grown up. He keeps behaving as if life were a game, but it isn't."

The waiter brought our pizzas, and my mother let him serve them in silence. When he left, she was lost in thought and didn't find her way back to me until she heard me pick up my cutlery.

"What was I saying?" she asked. "It doesn't matter . . . The important thing is for you not to worry. Papa worries much less than you or me, I can assure you. He started with what was easiest, that's all. If he really wants to do it, he'll have to make more of an effort . . . I don't think she would have even allowed me to invest."

My mother looked at me as if she were sounding out my reaction, smiled, then exclaimed, "Come on, let's eat."

She picked up her fork and knife to attack her pizza, and after I put the piece I had brought to my mouth back on the plate because it was too hot, I asked her:

"What if the same thing happens to me when I grow up?"

"What do you mean?"

"That I also won't know how to deal with responsibility."

My mother couldn't hide her amusement.

"It won't, I promise. And if it does, I hope you have a son as good as he has."

That conversation must have taken place on a Sunday in the middle of November, and we heard nothing more from my father until two weeks before Christmas. He called to find out what we would be doing on Christmas Eve. Our tradition—which his girlfriend had not altered, as she was not from Madrid and usually went out of town—was to celebrate with him and several branches of his family at his sister's house. My mother would not be able to join us this time, as she had already planned for her boyfriend to come to Madrid, and, partly to punish my father for this three-week silence and partly to appease my mother and her boyfriend, who continued to be apprehensive about any lingering effects on me of the fight with the glass, I decided to stay at home with them.

So it would have been if the weekend before Christmas vacation something hadn't happened that changed all our plans. On Friday, my mother and her boyfriend left me with the maid to go have dinner at the home of some friends who lived on the outskirts of Madrid, and by early Saturday morning they had still not returned. I found this out when the telephone woke me up and a woman, who did not identify herself and whose voice I did not recognize, asked me if there was an adult with me; when I said there wasn't, she was about to hang up, then thought better of it. She told me I mustn't worry, my mother was okay but had had an automobile accident near the town of Chinchón on her way back to Madrid in the early hours of the morning, and she was in a clinic there and would probably be transferred to a hospital. As soon as I hung up, and without losing my cool, I called my father; he said he would come immediately to pick me up so we could go to Chinchón together. I got dressed and went downstairs just as the maid was returning from walking the dog, carrying bread and the newspaper.

My father, who could never hide his emotions, soon showed up, urgency and worry writ large across his face. Without turning off the engine, he opened the passenger door then stepped on the gas without giving me time to close it. He didn't ask me how I was, and he didn't try to reassure me: he asked me to tell him every detail of the telephone conversation, exactly what they had said. After I finished, he didn't utter a word except to mention the traffic or the direction we should take at each fork in the road. I was glad for it. He behaved exactly as I expected him to. He seemed nervous and I was glad for that, as well. In the meantime, and as is my tendency whenever anything serious happens in my life, a strange calm came over me; it was as if I was observing the scene from outside. Not completely, though, for there was one question that kept going round and round in my head the whole way there. I wasn't able to pose it to my father until we had reached our destination.

"I know that Mama is okay," I stated with feigned conviction to give myself time to find the right words. "If not, they wouldn't have called me. They would have tried to find you. But, if one day something happens to her, would you take care of me?"

My father turned his eyes from the road to me, then released the steering wheel for a moment to pat my leg; again, he behaved exactly as I expected.

"Of course," he said, "what a question. But don't think about that because it will never be necessary."

Then, as silence enveloped us, I looked up and saw in the corner of the rearview mirror that his eyes were moist.

We rushed into the clinic and asked a guard for directions, then crossed paths with her boyfriend in the corridor on our way to my mother's room. He was limping, his glasses were broken, and his pants were torn, but it looked like he'd been only bruised. My father, who had never seen him, recognized him immediately, I suppose from the photo in my mother's bedroom, and blatantly, I would say almost scornfully, said not a word to him. Nor did my mother's boyfriend acknowledge my father: confused, ashamed, or perhaps because his head was bursting from a hangover, he only muttered a few words of apology as my father pressed his hand against my back to rush me past him.

My mother, who had been sitting in the passenger seat, was much more badly injured. Her head was wrapped in bandages that covered a cut on her forehead and one eye, from which they had extracted several pieces of glass; there was another bandage on one of her legs, where she had a fairly deep gash along the length of her shin. She was in bed, sedated, but she recognized us as soon as we approached.

"You are here, thank God," she said to both of us. "I was so worried. All I wanted was for them to sew me up and call you."

I don't remember the accident having any effect on my mother's spirits or altering her long-term plans with her boyfriend. At least she didn't say anything to me or show any outward signs of reconsidering anything; I also don't know what was discussed between them. I did, however, notice a change in him, a slight reticence toward me, as if he knew he'd been found out, which could also have been a response to my more pronounced distrust of him after the accident, a distrust that was abetted by my father. If until then he had bitten his tongue and only once allowed himself to say something against him, he now opened up the sluices and it poured forth whenever I gave him the chance. He blamed him for driving drunk. He said he was sick, called him an alcoholic, bad news, a vulgar man; he said that he didn't care about me, that he was a hypocrite and knew nothing about literature, that all the writers I told him he talked about were shit; he said my mother didn't know what she'd gotten herself into and that sooner or later it would all come crashing down.

That day of the accident, while we were following the ambulance that was carrying my mother to a hospital in Madrid, where we'd been told she would spend the night for observation, my father was more communicative than he had been on the way there. After listening to his first unprovoked attack on my mother's boyfriend, I brought up the subject of the publishing house he wanted to start and of my mother's refusal to give him the money, and he didn't shy away from talking about it.

"Your mother is the kindest person I know," he told me, "and that's as true now as it ever was. But this time I think she's wrong not to trust me. I can't blame her, though, not with my track record."

"She told me she doesn't have the money," I said, making excuses for her, "that she would have to ask for a loan from the bank, and she's afraid of having to pay it back. Can't you ask for one?" I asked.

"I can't get a loan. I don't have a salary or any assets, but don't worry. I'll figure something out."

My father spoke so dispassionately that it seemed to me he must be telling the truth. The traffic was sluggish. It must have been only a little past six o'clock, but it was getting dark and a certain crepuscular tone, which we could not entirely shake off, began to sink in. I suppose we were also feeling relieved after the strain of the trip there. I thought to ask him if his girlfriend could give him the money, but I didn't dare. We never mentioned her when we talked—it was as if she didn't exist. Still, it was in my head, and he must have noticed because he repeated:

"I'll get it somehow. Don't worry."

And then, as if talking to himself:

"I helped her with her store, and now it's doing really well."

It was obvious what he was talking about, and I didn't respond. Then he switched gears and asked me a question:

"So, have you decided what you're going to study?"

I told him I didn't know, that I still had five years before I had to decide.

"If you decide to write, don't make the mistake of getting a degree in literature. You can learn on your own everything they want to teach you. The only good it did me was that I met your mother."

I had never told him that I wanted to write; I read more than other kids my age, but if I was leaning toward anything it was history, and I was also drawn to archeology.

"Law would be good," he continued. "It exercises the mind. Or engineering. Look at Juan Benet. He's an engineer and a writer. I'd love to publish him. I'll mostly publish novels. Nobody reads essays. These days people want novels. There's a generation of good writers in their thirties who need to be heard. Can you imagine if in a few years from now I publish your first novel?"

My father kept talking about his future publishing venture until we pulled up behind the ambulance at the hospital where my mother was going to spend the night. I got out of the car and went in so I could say good-bye to her in her room, but he preferred to stay outside—my mother's boyfriend had been in the ambulance, and my father didn't want to cross paths with him again, afraid he'd punch him.

Half an hour later, my father took me home. When we turned onto my street, he asked me:

"Do you mind if I don't stay with you? Your mother's fine, there's nothing to worry about."

It was Saturday, around eight, the maid was off until Sunday afternoon, and he knew that my mother would not have wanted me to spend the night alone, but I said nothing, not wishing to give the impression that I was feeling resentful or trying to make him stay against his will. He said he'd call me the next day to take me to pick up my mother, but he didn't.

My mother's return home was arduous. It was difficult for her to walk because of the wound on her leg, and she had to wear a patch over her eye for several days. Her boyfriend, with unexpected aplomb, decided to return to France. She not only didn't object, she encouraged him to go. She preferred to convalesce alone and see him again after she had recovered. Proud as ever, I think that she preferred not to be seen in that condition. In any case, we spent Christmas Eve alone, not with her boyfriend, as we had planned, or with my father at his sister's. For the rest of the holidays, I accompanied her to the doctor for checkups and was her assistant and nurse all the many days the maid had off. There was time to talk, but we barely did. For instance, I longed for her to talk about the accident. I don't know what she was thinking, if a spark of trepidation about her boyfriend had been lit in her or if on the contrary she thought they had merely been victims of fate; in any case, her silence seemed strange and either it hid a concern she didn't dare share or she was still absorbing what had happened. My impression was that it was a little of both. I think she didn't believe in fate and blamed herself as much as she blamed her boyfriend; I think she considered that they both had been influenced by the exceptional nature of their time together as well as their shared penchant for partying and an active social life, and that they both had let themselves be carried away. I would even say that she thought that she enjoyed herself more and that he was looser, funnier, and more carefree when they were in that state, and that unconsciously she had not only encouraged him with her lack of concern for the consequences but that in a certain way she had spurred him on. He simply drank more and drove, she probably told herself.

My father didn't call me the entire month of January. Meanwhile, when my mother had fully recovered and only her scars were left to bear witness (the one on her leg could not be hidden, and the one on her forehead, thanks to the skill of the surgeon, was only a faint bluish line), her boyfriend came to Madrid two consecutive weekends. He had bought another car, the same model that had been in the accident, a somewhat sporty Peugeot convertible, and the first thing he said when he showed it to me was that he would give it to me when I turned eighteen. Though I might have been mistaken, I had the impression that they had talked and had come to some agreement. They went out less and returned home earlier, and they stuck to the prohibition, which they didn't mention but I noticed, against having alcohol at home. As for the rest, the decision for him to leave France the following semester and move in with us in Madrid remained firm. My mother would sell our apartment and, with an equal amount of money from him, they would buy a bigger apartment, where the three of us would have plenty of room. They decided to spend the summer together as a kind of dress rehearsal for their future life. We would not be guests at anybody's home, nor would we travel; we would rent a house for the month of August in a place where we didn't know anyone.

My father called the first weekend of February.

"I need you to do me a favor," he said. "I need you to help me move some things and store them at your place for a while. I don't think your mother will mind; there's not much."

I explained that my mother's boyfriend was with us and that he would be staying until Sunday.

"Okay, then, Monday. Tell your mother I'll pick you up at school and we'll be back before dinner."

On Monday, my father was actually waiting for me when I got out of school. He smiled and gave me a kiss, as if we'd just seen each other the day before, and he took me to a house I'd never seen before but that I'd tried to imagine many times.

"We have to be quick about it," he said, rushing me.

He took down some paintings, filled five or six boxes with books, shoved some clothes into two suitcases, wrapped several objects in newspaper then put them in plastic bags, grabbed a table lamp and a large wicker basket he first had to empty of old newspapers, and when he had everything piled next to the door, he said:

"I'm leaving a lot here, and I'm only taking what's most important."

My mother was curious and concerned when she greeted us, but after finding out what was going on, she did not hide her agitation. My father, who had still not given me any explanation on the way to the house, did not refuse her one.

"It's only for a little while," he said, "until I find an apartment."

"And you, where will you live in the meantime?" my mother asked.

"With my business partner."

My mother gave him a stern look, and for a moment I feared that they would have one of those fights that used to be so frequent when my father still lived with us, when his anarchic tendencies, his acting without thinking and without taking other people into account, hit up against my mother's sense of order, her need to subject everything to an exacting discipline. That need, not an intrinsic part of her character but rather manifested reluctantly within the context of her life with my father, was sometimes despotically applied where it didn't belong.

"Your partner?"

"Yes, we're moving forward with the publishing house," he answered. "Right now I'll start as a consultant, and later, when I get the money . . . "

"What happened?" my mother cut in. "Didn't she give it to you?"

My mother had posed the question already knowing the answer, and that was the turning point that could have eroded my desire for him to feel our support. That did not happen, thanks to him either not perceiving the sting in my mother's words or not wanting to take it into account, knowing above all that it was the result of the bewilderment she suffered whenever confronted with something unforeseen. His reaction was even more unexpected. He confessed that the woman he had considered until very recently his partner, and about whom we never spoke, had indeed refused to give him money; he referred to her with very harsh words like *greedy* and *money-grubbing*, then he suddenly fell apart as I had never seem him do before. It was obvious that the bluster of his earlier diatribe was feigned and that he was much more affected than he had at first tried to pretend.

"I don't understand," he admitted, while my mother was rubbing his back to comfort him. "I helped her when my situation was worse than hers. I gave her everything I had so she could start her business, and now that she's doing so well, she refuses to lend me a lot less money than I gave her. I don't understand. I'm surprised. I'm also offended. What hurts most is that I trusted her. Though I always knew I couldn't, not in certain ways. She's insecure, obstinate, and she's very jealous. She can't understand why I keep coming here. Anything that has anything to do with you two, even the most basic, really sets her off. But I thought she loved me and that being with me was what was most important to her . . . "

Neither my mother nor I said anything despite both of us wanting to. It did not make sense to pour salt on his wounds, not if it was over. My mother, still rubbing his back, stopped, and moments later, while we were still standing there in silence, she pointed to the packages that we had piled by the door, and said:

"Come on, let's put this stuff away." Then, once we moved into action, she turned to my father and said, "You're staying for dinner, aren't you?"

The following five months were the longest and strangest that I ever spent with my parents. The same night I have just described, when we finished eating, my mother invited my father to stay the night.

"Today, and for as long as you want," she specified, "until you find an apartment and start working again. It doesn't make sense for you to stay with your partner. It could cause tension, and that could hurt your publishing plans."

Some might deduce from my mother's generous invitation that she planned to seduce my father or that she wanted at least to share her life with him again, but they would be wrong. My father accepted the invitation to stay at the house—which was, I think, what he had really hoped for all along—and she immediately started thinking about her boyfriend, not how to leave him or how to let him know about our hospitality toward my father, but rather how to hide it from him so as not to upset him.

"The next few times I'll have to go to France instead of him coming here," she said, as if talking to herself. "Oh, and you are forbidden from answering the phone," she warned my father. Next, turning lightheartedly to the two of us, she said, "This isn't exactly normal, you know. He'd have a very hard time understanding." Then, again, to my father: "You'd better start working soon and find an apartment right away."

The complicity those words revealed never faltered, in spite of the fact that the so-called state of emergency lasted much longer than expected. While my father's employment situation was stalled, my mother went to France at the end of February, and again in March—for Easter week—then again in May. During all those trips,

I stayed with my father. We had never been so close. I suspect he was depressed, for he barely left the house (he was there when I woke up, when I returned home from school, and when I went to bed), but I think that his unqualified acceptance of a domestic order he had been so unwilling to accept in the past had nothing to do with it. That acceptance could be explained by something more than his gratitude toward my mother, which he expressed in thousands of ways. I think he was touched by the opportunity to spend that time with us, to get to know us from close up; I think he liked our company, and the idyllic harmony we achieved together was in great part due to the ease with which he made everything he could flow so smoothly. I don't know if he ever played with the idea that his stay would become permanent, if he dismissed the possibility or harbored any illusions about it. We never mentioned a future different from the one set forth at the beginning of his stay. Even if we had wanted to, we never dared. My mother talked to her boyfriend almost daily, there was always a trip to France in the works, and it was difficult to forget that our situation was quite out of the ordinary. As far as her feelings, the explanation is more complex. I am certain that *she* harbored no illusions about making a temporary situation permanent, that she didn't even fantasize about it, for the simple reason that she did not allow herself to envisage it. Which—I can't help thinking—had less to do with an iron sense of commitment or an unbreakable loyalty to her boyfriend and more with the pain the slow deterioration of her past life with my father still caused her. I have a feeling that after their separation, after the relief that followed the initial dismay and the diffident and failed attempts with other men who came and went, who either demanded too much from her or did not give her what she expected, she had needed so badly to establish a relationship that when she finally had one that seemed to fulfill her expectations, she safeguarded it against any and all contingencies, even her own doubts.

I don't think my mother believed that my father had changed. I think she knew that his love for her, like hers for him, was greater than anything either of them could feel for anybody else, but she was always aware of the excessive liberties—which my father had generously taken—that this kind of unconditional love affords those who become aware of its unconditional nature, and subsequently give the fluctuations of their own moods too wide a berth.

The fact is that not one of the three of us, not even I, dared to consider a future together—my mother's plans being what they were—but one can nevertheless say that we lived with our backs to everything that was not daily life. This is the only way to explain that the passing of time didn't alarm us, that we were not in any rush. This is the only way to explain that when it became obvious that my father's publishing venture was not going to take off unless he invested his share, my mother did not pressure him. She offered to give him the money when she had it, my father spoke to us about a place for rent in an old industrial building downtown where he wanted to set up the office, he told us that his partner had agreed that he could use part of it as a living space, and he even suggested I come live with him, but these and other references to a later time were mentioned without urgency, leaving the moment for decision up in the air. In this way, almost without talking about it, it became settled that my mother would give my father the money he needed when we sold our house in the fall and that, before leaving in August to spend the summer vacation with her boyfriend, she would give him a certain amount of money to rent the place and start on the necessary renovations. I think my mother was worried; I think she, like I, saw my father as fragile and depressed, and it is likely that she was unwilling to rush him. It is also likely that they spoke behind my back and came to an agreement. As far as he was concerned, and considering his status as a guest, it seemed normal for him to submit to the rhythm imposed by others.

Another possibility occurs to me now, though I consider it quite remote, almost impossible, and not in keeping with her straightforward personality, and this is that my mother's apparent lack of concern about the passing of time, the fact that she neither nagged my father nor pressured him to make a decision, was the result of an ulterior motive: to avoid burning her bridges with him until she found out during her summer experiment if her relationship with her boyfriend was going to work out.

No, I definitely don't think that possible.

In June, with summer approaching, my mother found no more excuses to travel to France and had to agree that her boyfriend would come to Madrid for a few days. We removed all traces of my father from the house, and he and I got out of the way by going to Lisbon for the weekend. My mother's boyfriend returned at the beginning of July, and this time, my father took refuge at his sister's house. At the end of the month, he had to disappear one last time while my mother and I welcomed her boyfriend and, a few days later, already in August, the three of us left for the Basque Country, where we had rented a house.

We would take the night train, my mother's boyfriend's convertible carried in the train's car transporter. I spent the whole last day with my father, then returned home in the evening to go to the station. He seemed sad, or shy, as if he couldn't decide if he should tell me things he dared not, or perhaps the sad and shy one was me because I didn't know how to say what I felt. Or we both were. We ate lunch at a Chinese restaurant, more silent than talkative, and then we wandered for a while through the streets under the withering sun. We didn't have enough time to go to a movie, so we ended up taking refuge at an exhibit at the National Archeological Museum. We left and started walking home. My father suggested he wait at the pub below until it was time for us to leave, then he would go upstairs and stay in the house, keeping an eye on the renovations at the publishing house, until we returned the first of September. As I still had a little time, I wanted to go with him to the pub. He opened the door for me, and as I started to enter, he held his other arm out to stop me in my tracks.

"Look," he said.

I saw my mother's boyfriend sitting on a stool at the bar. He was clumsily trying to take some money out of his wallet to pay the waiter, who was watching him impatiently, and we were able to withdraw without him seeing us.

"He must have just dropped his car off at the station," I said without conviction, and I suppose in order to prevent my father from observing him too closely. "He had to bring it early so they could load it on the train."

"Yeah, of course," my father answered as he placed his hand on my head and rushed me across the street, "and he was thirsty."

That was the first ironic comment he had allowed himself since, five months earlier, my mother and I had welcomed him into the house, and he said nothing more; he didn't insist. We waited a few minutes on the sidewalk across the street, hidden behind a bus stop, and when we saw my mother's boyfriend leave and enter the house, we returned to the pub. My father didn't want me to stay with him any longer. He took two packages out of a plastic bag he had told me before carried his razor and toiletries, and handed them to me.

"Here," he said. "A journal to write in and a book to inspire you."

The journal was a Chinese calligraphy notebook, and the book was *Nine Stories*, by Salinger. Then we said good-bye. As I turned to go into the house, the last thing I heard him say was:

"Take care of your mother."

Tears were running down my cheeks, and I didn't dare turn to look at him because I knew that he would be crying, too.

For the first few days in the Basque Country, I couldn't get out of my head an image that was not real, for it had not happened, but it did sum up my state of mind: my father furtively saying good-bye to me while the taxi that we had taken to the station drove off, leaving him behind.

As to what we really did, how we spent those first days of August, I remember, on the contrary, very little.

I do remember our arrival. I remember the slightly exaggerated delight with which my mother tried to cheer me up when we entered the house and looked around; I remember her organizational fervor, our first trip to buy groceries, our scouting around for shops; I remember the already familiar ritual from other summers in other places we rented: her determination to throw out all the cleaning equipment and buy new, and the alcohol to clean the toilets, which she then lit on fire to disinfect them; I remember that I didn't like my bedroom, dark and with two bunk beds; and I remember going to look for the way to the beach. My mother and I did all these things alone while her boyfriend explored the house on his own, meticulously unpacked his bags, and began to work on an essay about the writers of the Latin American literary boom. I remember there were frustrated negotiations about which room he would work in, about how he inexplicably wanted the kitchen. My mother, who exchanged with me a look of stupefaction, attempted to dissuade him, but he argued that he needed light, and there was more of it in the kitchen than anywhere else.

"But what will happen when I'm preparing food?" my mother insisted. "Or if we want to have a snack? We'll disturb you."

He didn't answer, but the expression on his face made it obvious that such a possibility had never occurred to him. Then, in a show of force that surprised me, he opened the folding table and placed his typewriter and a lectern on top of it. All of this would have been merely one incident in the collection of that summer's unusual events if it had taken my mother and I only two days to discover that, as she had feared, we really were not welcome in the kitchen while he was working. The looks of annoyance, or contained rage, he gave us for any necessary incursion into his domain were in no way ambiguous.

After this first exchange, my recollections become evanescent, the memories blend together, and I start to lose the chronological thread. Except for the submerged crescendo of tension, the days were all the same, one barely distinguishable from the other because everything was organized around my mother's boyfriend's work schedule. He usually rose very early, around five thirty. I know because the sound of his street shoes, which he wore at that hour of the day without socks, woke me up almost every morning. For this reason, and because sometimes I came out of my room before trying to fall back to sleep, I also knew that he did squats and then read for two hours, stretched out on the sofa in the living room. Next, he'd go into the kitchen to write and, from then until nine at night when he called it a day, he took three breaks, as far as I know: one around twelve, when he got dressed and went out for half an hour, another for lunch and to take a short nap, and the last around seven, when he went out again. Neither then nor in the morning did my mother and I accompany him. Family life, if you could call it that, took place at lunch and, above all, at dinner and after dinner. My mother and I spent the rest of the time alone. We went to the beach or, if it was raining, something it started doing with despairing frequency, we took a taxi and escaped to San Sebastián to go to the movies, always with the sensation, aggravated by the cold receptions we subsequently received, that this separate life we were living also displeased her boyfriend, that even though he was working in the kitchen, he preferred to have us nearby.

Ten hours, which is what my mother and I spent together on most days, goes a long way, especially if the surrounding reality offers an unexpected vein to be mined or there is a third party who does everything possible to become the center of attention. It took my mother and me some time, however, to verbalize our involuntary alliance, which strengthened as her boyfriend's peculiarities proliferated. We pretended, we averted our eyes. Pride held us back, and it is likely that she was trying to protect him during what could have been a temporary disturbance and that I was trying to support her. Or that she felt ashamed or guilty, obliged to offer me an explanation she didn't know how to formulate, and that her embarrassment made me feel sorry for her.

Thanks to the trust that neither she nor I wanted to see proscribed, we were able to restrain ourselves, and there were days, especially at the beginning, when in spite of the ever narrower margin of possibilities, he was capable of reigniting embers of past cheerfulness. I can recall nights when the living room was filled with laughter, though mostly I remember him stern and vigilant, as if he were waging a fierce battle against an aggressive and invisible army of which my mother and I were the fifth column. If she or I expressed an opinion on any subject whatsoever, and the other agreed, a disproportionate response was immediately forthcoming. Sometimes we didn't even need to agree with each other, it was enough that one of us disagreed with him for him to bitterly recriminate both of us. There were occasions, such as one lunchtime when he rebuked my mother for what he called her rude habit of dipping her bread in the sauce of the stew and then lifting her plate to her lips to drink from it directly, when we felt so overwhelmed by the sensation of being unwilling actors in a comedic play that we could not stop ourselves from laughing with foolhardy audacity.

The conviction that there was no reasonable explanation for what we were experiencing, that it was not a result of mere confusion due to stress or some other cause but rather something more serious and intractable, slowly pervaded us. The odd thing is that this certainty, once firmly established, did not liberate us or make it any easier to cut off; on the contrary, our servitude increased, turning us into prisoners of pity. We not only submitted passively to his delirium but we had learned how to apologize for faults we had not committed. It was this contradiction that finally made it easier for my mother to talk to me. She chose a trip in a taxi on the way to San Sebastián, after a morning when her boyfriend, offended by who knows what imagined offense, had not uttered a word to either of us.

"We're going to put up with it," she said. "We are not going to return to Madrid defeated."

I think she was afraid that if there was a sudden rupture, he would lose whatever control he still wielded over himself, and, as the summer would soon be over, she thought it better to leave him once and for all after we returned to Madrid and he to France.

More than twenty-five years have passed since then and I still wonder what led to the final explosion. It is clear that ever since the automobile accident in Chinchón, his concealment of his dependence on alcohol, which I assume made him drink more anxiously in less time, was at the root of everything. That was, let us say, the fuse. As far as the fuel, I can only speculate: perhaps his insecurity about the extent of my mother's commitment, perhaps his secret rivalry with me that he thought he'd lost, perhaps the shadow of my father, perhaps his inability to live with others, perhaps a conflict wholly within himself. Who knows. The rest, the spreading of the flames, was in the hands of the winds—a whirlwind of sensitivities and misunderstandings that created a spontaneous feedback loop. The isolation he forced himself into in order to work, the strong likelihood that it was going badly, his distorted perception of the complicity between my mother and me . . .

The month of August 1983 began like every other August in the north of the country, with uncertainty about the number of beach days it would provide, but that year it ended in catastrophe. Around the middle of the month, the sky clouded over and it did not stop raining until torrential rains on the twenty-sixth paralyzed everything and caused major flooding throughout Vizcaya, in most of Guipúzcoa, and in some parts of Álva. The flooding of the Nervión River, in Bilbao, caused many deaths and several disappearances. Apparently, the phenomenon was set off by a front of cold air from the north colliding at a great altitude with warm air from the south, though other theories attributed it to a storm of tropical origin. We were on the San Sebastián side, in Fuenterrabía, and were not that badly affected. We were subjected to the rain, we spent nights in awe listening to the sky being torn to pieces, but there was no flooding nearby.

The disaster occurred the day we had planned to leave, but by then we were already safe. My mother reached her limit one afternoon when we found the door to the apartment open and her boyfriend, who greeted us in a state of drunken agitation, accusing her of cheating on him and going to San Sebastián to meet someone; he called her an adulteress, mentioned the word *incest*, and I don't know how much other nonsense. For at least an hour, after taking refuge in my room on my mother's orders, I heard shouts and slamming doors alternating with short bouts of whispering. Then, just when it seemed that neither of them was going to give up, I heard my mother say above the storm raging outside, in a silence like that between a bolt of lightning and the thunderclap it announces, *It's okay, it's okay*, and I heard him sobbing. A short time later, my mother opened the door to my room and asked me to go to him. I found him in bed, his face more anguished than ever, trying to take two pills out of a bottle of Valium. Without hesitating, without even looking at my mother, I helped him with the pills, handed him a glass of water from the bedside table, and, while he was apologizing, held his hand and stroked it, telling him that everything was okay, that he mustn't worry. Then I went back to my room.

"Pack your bags quietly," my mother told me when she reappeared, twenty minutes to a half hour later. "We're leaving."

My mother was completely silent in the taxi that took us to San Sebastián and spoke only when absolutely necessary in the hotel where we spent what remained of the night. She seemed tired and vulnerable. Having lost her characteristic and legendary self-assurance, she did not open the suitcase even to take out her toiletries. She got undressed in the bathroom, and instead of walking to the head of the bed to get in, she crawled to the foot of the bed and did a complicated somersault that left her for a moment with her legs and arms in the air.

The next day we tried to buy an airplane ticket, but the airport was closed because of the storm. We caught the first train to Madrid. For a while we watched through the window as the city slowly disintegrated and made room for the countryside: the housing blocks in the suburbs, the small industrial zone, and then the rolling green hills sprinkled with clusters of farmhouses . . . Just when I was starting to think about my mother's boyfriend, if he had woken up and discovered our flight, what he would do when he did, if he would try to get her back and how he would take the rejection that I now took for a certainty, my mother started talking about her childhood summers spent in a very similar landscape to the one we were riding through, about her grandfather's house in León, the games she played with her cousins, the neighbors, the farm work, the advantages of rural life, and anything else that came into her head. Afterward, when it seemed she couldn't find any more material to sustain her monologue, she tried to find a comfortable position, leaned her head back, and closed her eyes.

"We're going back to your father," she whispered, almost to herself, in a voice that was, nonetheless, hers again.

I already knew, because I had intuited it the moment we had said good-bye, and had corroborated it when I had called him to no avail from many phone booths that summer, that my father would not be waiting for us at home, but I did not tell her. I preferred that she sleep. For a while, I continued looking at the landscape that was losing—the further south we went and the clearer the sky—that leaden quality that is a prelude to storms, and I let my thoughts wander. I thought about my father and my mother, about each of them separately and the two of them together; I thought about the intense months we were leaving behind; I asked myself if everything hadn't turned out for the best, if it wasn't better, after all was said and done, that my father would not be waiting for us at home; I thought about the coming academic year; I wondered if there would be someone among my classmates whom I could tell about what I had just lived; I thought about our house, the one we would no longer be moving out of; I thought about my dog, whom we had left at the boarder's; I remembered the maid, who would still have a few days left of vacation, and then I also fell asleep.

Marcos Giralt Torrente was born in Madrid in 1968 and is the author of three novels, a novella, and a book of short stories. He was writer-in-residence at the Spanish Academy in Rome, the Künstlerhaus Schloss Wiepersdorf, and the University of Aberdeen, and was part of the Berlin Artists-in-Residence Programme in 2002–2003. He is the recipient of several distinguished awards, most importantly the Spanish National Book Award in 2011. His works have been translated into French, German, Greek, Italian, Korean and Portuguese. *The End of Love* is his first book to appear in English.

Katherine Silver is an award-winning translator of Spanish and Latin American literature. Her most recent translations include works by Daniel Sada, Horacio Castellanos Moya, and César Aira. She is the co-director of the Banff International Literary Translation Centre in Canada and lives in Berkeley, California.